Henry John Stephen Smith

Biographical Sketches and Recollections

(with early letters) of Henry John Stephen Smith

Henry John Stephen Smith

Biographical Sketches and Recollections
(with early letters) of Henry John Stephen Smith

ISBN/EAN: 9783337077648

Printed in Europe, USA, Canada, Australia, Japan

Cover: Foto ©Raphael Reischuk / pixelio.de

More available books at **www.hansebooks.com**

Henry J Smith

AND

RECOLLECTIONS

(*WITH EARLY LETTERS*)

OF

HENRY JOHN STEPHEN SMITH

M.A., F.R.S.

LATE SAVILIAN PROFESSOR OF GEOMETRY IN THE UNIVERSITY OF OXFORD

WITH A PORTRAIT

PRINTED FOR PRIVATE CIRCULATION

M DCCC XCIV

Oxford
HORACE HART, PRINTER TO THE UNIVERSITY

CONTENTS

BIOGRAPHICAL SKETCH

THE short record of Henry Smith's life, which I have compiled at the request of his sister, is chiefly based upon a Memoir by herself, which I was anxious to give in its entirety, but for which she has desired me to substitute my own words. I have to thank Professor Irving for a letter containing his recollections of Henry Smith at Balliol in his first years as Fellow and Lecturer. The Memoir and Letters from which I have worked are unfortunately most defective during the years of my own absence from England, 1871–1883; and I must ask my readers to bear in mind under what disadvantages I have attempted to perform a sacred duty. Happily, Henry Smith's character, about which there is really no difference of opinion, exhibits an unbroken continuity of growth. As a boy he seemed to have something of the mature wisdom of a man; and to the day of his death he retained the simplicity and high spirits of a boy. My own estimate of him, based on the close intimacy of more than twenty years, represents, I hope and believe, what his friends thought and would wish said. To those who did not know him, it will perhaps appear that my judgment has been influenced by friendship. Those who knew him will notice points I have missed or excellences I have slurred, and will condemn my inadequacy.

The original plan of this Memoir assumed that it would be supplemented by the publication of a large number of Henry Smith's letters. This was over-ruled in Oxford while I was in Australia, and cannot now be reverted to. Of these letters a few only have been published. Neither, unfortunately,

b

have I leisure or strength to recast the Memoir altogether.   I have done
what I can in that direction, and can only hope that the difficulties under
which I have worked may be borne in mind.

CHARLES H. PEARSON*.

MELBOURNE, 1888.
LONDON, 1893.

HENRY JOHN STEPHEN SMITH was the second son of John Smith,
a distinguished though short-lived Irish barrister, who, after graduating at
Trinity College, Dublin, was law pupil, at the Temple, of Serjeant Henry John
Stephen, the learned editor of Blackstone's Commentaries. Mr. John Smith went
back to practise in Dublin, and in 1818 married Mary Murphy. By this marriage
he had four children—a daughter, who died of consumption in 1834 at the age
of fifteen; a son, Charles, who died also of consumption in 1843, being then
a cadet at Addiscombe; a daughter who still lives; and the subject of this
Memoir, who was named after his father's old tutor, and who was born on the
2nd of November, 1826.

Mr. Smith died in 1828, of abscess of the liver, and his widow was left for
a time in very straitened circumstances. Fortunately, after delays which seemed
interminable, the Courts affirmed the validity of a bequest of £10,000, which
had been made to Mr. Smith by his cousin the Marchioness of Ormond, and
which her husband disputed. With this money, and with that produced by
the sale of a house which Mr. Smith had just built, the widow had wherewithal
to provide adequately for her family; and partly to escape from sorrowful asso-
ciations, partly to secure for her children that good education which it had been
their father's earnest wish they should receive, Mrs. Smith resolved within
six months of her husband's death to pass over into England. The family
wandered successively to the Isle of Man, 1829; to Harborne near Birmingham,
1829-30; to Leamington, 1830-31; and then to Ryde in the Isle of Wight,
where nine or ten years were spent.

Probably no widow left in charge of a young family could have been better
fitted to train them for eminence in after life than was Mrs. Smith. A tall

---

* Dr. Pearson's death has deprived this 'Sketch' of the benefit of the author's final revision.

distinguished-looking lady, who retained the traces of great beauty to the day of her death, and who united a certain stateliness of manner and reserve of temperament to Irish ease and kindly charm of manner, she was also considerably more than an accomplished and clever woman, for she possessed powers and learning such as are rare even among able and learned men. Henry Smith inherited genius on both sides. He was a sickly child, and he was also short-sighted from a very early age, perhaps partly from being allowed to read too much when he was quite young. In 1831, when he was only four years old, he was able to follow English and French lessons. He also picked up an old Greek grammar of his mother's, rendered additionally formidable by contractions, and learned the alphabet, the nouns, the adjectives and the pronouns for his own pleasure. 'His practice,' says his sister, 'was to lay himself at full length on his stomach on the floor with the book he wished to study under his chin to suit his sight. When he was between seven and eight I remember Prideaux' *Connection* being for long an absorbing study.' As soon as his mother found out how marked his taste for language was, she took him into her own hands for the classics, and for the next six or seven years he owed all his chief training to her. In 1838 the pupil had got so far that his mother thought it desirable to call in other aid. She was fortunate enough to meet with a highly trained tutor in the person of Mr. R. Wheler Bush, who has put his recollections of Henry Smith on record in the following terms :

'In the years 1838–39 Henry Smith, then a boy of eleven years of age, read with me for about nine months at Ryde, in the Isle of Wight. He had been previously taught by his widowed mother—a remarkably clever and highly educated woman. After reading with Henry Smith I had a large experience of boys during a head-mastership of more than thirty-three years, but I have often remarked that the brilliant talents of Henry Smith prevented me from ever being really astonished at the abilities of any subsequent pupil. His power of memory, quickness of perception, indefatigable diligence, and intuitive grasp of whatever he studied were very remarkable at that early age. What he got through during those few months, and the way in which he got through it, have never ceased to surprise me. From a record which I have before me I see that during that short time he read all Thucydides, Sophocles, and Sallust, twelve books of Tacitus, the greater part of Horace, Juvenal, Persius, and several plays of Æschylus and Euripides. I see also that he got up six books of Euclid, and algebra to simple equations; that he read a considerable quantity of Hebrew; and that, among other things, he learnt all the Odes of Horace by heart. I could scarcely understand at the time how he contrived at his early age to translate so well and so accurately the most difficult speeches of Thucydides, without note or comment to guide him. He was a deeply interesting boy, singularly modest, lovable, and affectionate.' (*Times*, Feb. 12, 1883.)

Scarcely less valuable for the boy's development were the abundant leisure that he enjoyed, and the comparative isolation. His lessons never occupied more than five hours a day, and the obligatory 'constitutional' was only of an hour. During the rest of the time the brothers and sisters were turned out to play by themselves. Their story books were limited to *Robinson Crusoe, Evenings at Home, Sandford and Merton*, and Miss Edgeworth's *Frank*; their toys consisted of hoops and tops, and one or two dissected games. They grew up like the young Brontës, in a world of their own, improvising plays from *Robinson Crusoe* or combats from Homer. In one of these fights Henry had his finger badly hurt by an arrow from the bow of Achilles, his elder brother, and the surgeon's aid had to be called in. These amusements could not occupy their whole leisure. In idle hours the children became diligent students of animal and insect life, learning much about the habits of bees and ants and spiders and wood-lice and garden moths. They were directed in these pursuits by two books, *Insect Architecture* and *Insect Transformations*, from the Library of Entertaining and Useful Knowledge, and assisted in them by two neighbours, a lady who was something of a botanist and a conchologist, and a Mr. Jacques, who had some knowledge of chemistry. That the interest they took in these matters was more than cursory seems proved by the fact that they supplied Dr. Blomfield, who was engaged on a Flora of the Isle of Wight, with several new homes of rare plants.

In 1839 Mr. Bush was called away to a head-mastership. It proved difficult to supply his place, though an excellent mathematical master was found at Newport, who came over twice a week and carried his pupils through the advanced parts of Arithmetic, elementary Algebra, and Euclid. Henry continued to be a very docile pupil, sometimes asking, when he received an order which displeased him, whether he was 'forced' to obey it, but never demurring if he understood that obedience was required. In 1840, however, he lost his chief fellow-student, through his elder brother going to Addiscombe, and Mrs. Smith decided on moving to Oxford, where it was certain that better teaching could be found than in the Isle of Wight. The Oxford of those days was comparatively a small place. Resident professors, married tutors, and married fellows were almost or quite unknown, while the Heads of Houses, then the governing body of the University, formed a little society of their own. Consequently, the widow lived in comparative solitude, though even so she could not avoid hearing something of the war of opinion that was beginning : of the angry opposition provoked by Tract 90, of Newman's sermons, of the coalition of Evangelicals and Liberals against Puseyites, and now and again of the few Liberals who stood outside the strife of the Churches. Meanwhile she had been exceptionally fortunate in the tutor she secured for her son. The Rev. Henry Highton, Fellow of Queen's and then Curate of St. Ebbe's, was a sound though not a brilliant scholar, and a really good mathematician, far above the average of Oxford in those days. No one could be better fitted to develop Henry Smith's varied capacities, and in Mr. Highton's class-room Henry, for the first time, was able to measure himself with boys of his own age. In the summer of 1841 Mr. Highton received the offer of a Mastership at Rugby, which at that time was chiefly valuable when a boarding-house was attached to it. Mr. Highton accepted the offer, which allowed of his marrying, and proposed that he should take Henry Smith with him as his first boarder. Mrs. Smith agreed, and Henry was thus launched into school life under the most famous teacher of the day, Dr. Arnold.

I have always regarded it as singularly fortunate for Henry Smith that he was at Rugby in its best days, and that he was not there long enough to acquire that part of its tone which was not generally popular. Whether that sweet buoyant nature, with its supreme sense of proportion, and lively humour, could ever have been really spoiled, made pedantic or harsh, is perhaps more than doubtful ; but I cannot doubt that the years of travel on the Continent, which two chances, that seemed unkindly, substituted for school and Oxford life, were really of the greatest use to the sufferer. He carried on his studies abroad less methodically, but quite as profitably, as he could have done at home ; he learned French, German, and Italian, and he gained some acquaintance with foreign ideas and methods. Meanwhile his first years at Rugby were certainly profitable to him. It was a rule of the school that no one should be in the Sixth Form until he was sixteen, and in deference to this rule

Henry Smith was kept for a year doing work below his capacity in the Upper Fifth and the Twenty Form, though by a curious anomaly he was allowed to act as præpostor in Mr. Highton's house, where he was the senior boy. His Report for the first half-year, which was spent in the Fifth Form, has been preserved ; and might have been written of him at almost any time :—' *Classics* : In extent and variety of knowledge he is certainly the best in the Form, and he is **particularly** **fortunate** in combining accurate and literal construing with an excellent choice of English words. His composition also (though it has sometimes been careless) is spirited and clever. *Mathematics* : **Very good.** *Modern Languages* : **He has** **made great** progress in German, and is getting on very well. **He has been late** for morning prayers oftener than I like ; and I should wish him to get rid of a few trifling irregularities, such as occasional inattention at lesson and inaccuracy in saying his lines. G. E. L. COTTON, Master of the Fifth Form.' When in the Twenty he came under Mr. (afterwards Professor) Bonamy Price, con-fessedly the ablest teacher on the very able staff of which Rugby then boasted, and probably never surpassed as a teacher of classics. In the Midsummer exam-ination of that year, Henry Smith passed into the **Sixth, and was accordingly** entitled to bid the Doctor good-bye. **A few days later he received a letter from** Mr. Highton (June 12) :—' You hardly supposed that **when you bid Dr. Arnold** " good-bye" on Friday it was for the last time. **He was taken to his rest at six** this morning. . . . You may imagine how the loss is felt here. It is almost as if a common parent were taken away. I felt it so quite myself.'

The true education of a boy at a public school is even more in the play-ground than in the class-room. What Henry Smith was in this regard has not come down to me. Going to Rugby just before he left it, I remember to have heard ' Highton Smith,' as he was popularly called, spoken of with vague reverence for his great ability, but in no other way. Nevertheless there are indications from reports and letters that he was abundantly capable of healthy enjoyment, and not merely what the Rugbeans used to call a ' swat ' or book-worm. Mr. Highton twice reports of him in his first half-year that he was not working as hard as he ought ; and his sister says that ' he came home for his first holidays "astonishing" us by the buoyancy of his spirits and even more by a propensity for " grub," unknown to the ascetic days of his childhood. By one who learned so easily as he did, a little idleness was easily made up for.' In the examination of June 1843 he obtained a Junior Scholarship, being ineligible for the University Scholarship because he had not been three years in the school. In July 1843 the new head master, Dr. Tait, wrote to Mrs. Smith to say :—' There is no young man in the Sixth Form from whose abilities I am led to expect more than from him ; and . . . . . I have formed a very high opinion of his character and conduct generally.'

Rugby however was not to keep him. In September 1843 his elder brother Charles died of rapid consumption, and the uncle, who was also guardian and adviser, declined under these circumstances to consent to Henry's remaining any longer at a school in a bleak part of England. The boy bore the blow to his ambition with his unvarying sweetness, and wintered with his family at Nice, while he spent the following summer by the Lake of Lucerne. These were months of steady reading, though his books were few, and he was even unprovided with a Greek lexicon. In the autumn of 1844 he went back to his old friend, Mr. Highton, for a month, that he might be 'coached' for the Balliol scholarship. He won it easily, and, as he was not to go into residence till Easter, went back to join his family at Rome. His journey was a series of disasters. He missed the mail-boat at Dover, had his pocket picked at Paris, and, even after pledging his books, could only muster funds enough to carry him in the roughest way to Rome. This misadventure involved a journey of seventy hours, on the outside of a diligence during a severe frost, to Marseilles ; and, after a third-class passage from that port to Civita Vecchia, he arrived in Rome with both his feet frost-bitten, and was laid up for a long time. Presently came an attack of small-pox. 'All the same,' writes his sister, 'the winter was a time of intense enjoyment, and a gathering and growing time.' By Easter he was well enough to go to Oxford, and spend his first term there.

When the Long Vacation came Henry Smith rejoined his mother and sister in Italy. Unfortunately they arranged to spend the summer at Frascati in the Alban Hills, and Henry soon became languid and ailing, and at last ill enough to need a doctor. The doctor who came, an Italian physician of eminence, declared after three weeks that his patient was undoubtedly consumptive, and ordered him to the sea at Naples by way of the Pontine Marshes. Even in their alarm the family were discreet enough to substitute the hill route for the deadly road along the plains ; but this involved a four days' journey, during which the sufferer became delirious, and, when Naples was at length reached, the English doctors had all left the city. One however was to be found at Castellamare, and he, when he was called in, declared that the disease was nothing but long-neglected malaria, which an ordinary Italian doctor should have recognised. It was now thought right to revert to the use of strong tonics. Severe inflammatory attacks subsequently came on. These have been, since then, attributed to the presence of gall-stones, which may have possibly laid the foundation of his latest illness. Moreover, with spring (1845), the malaria itself returned, and it became necessary to leave the South. He himself at a later time described his illness to me as a sort of euthanasia, in which he seemed to be gliding painlessly out of life. The sister who helped to nurse him remembers that he was too weak even to put up his glass that he might look at an eruption of Mount Vesuvius. Still he was able to enjoy being read aloud to, and his mother used to read to him incessantly from English newspapers and standard authors, but especially from the Latin and Greek classics, while on Sundays he would honour the day by forbearing to correct or even to shudder at a false quantity. The move from Naples was to Wiesbaden, and there the waters restored him to comparative health. It was thought better however that he should not return to England, and accordingly the next winter (1845–6) was spent at Paris, where Henry Smith attended several of the courses at the College of France or the Sorbonne, and derived especial advantages from the lectures of Arago and of Milne Edwards. By this time his strength was thoroughly re-established, and, though he went a second time to Wiesbaden in the summer of 1847, he had already resumed work at Oxford (Easter, 1847), and never afterwards needed to suspend it. His health, as I remember it for more than twenty years of unbroken intimacy, during which I was constantly seeing him, was always good, though never what could be called robust. He suffered especially as a young man from weak eyes; and he had to be a little careful of himself in diet and exercise; but he was rarely depressed, and he habitually worked beyond what most men could have endured without breaking down. There was one attack of low fever in 1856, the result of course of the earlier Roman fever, in consequence of which he was ordered to ride, and the obligation to take horse exercise was undoubtedly very good for him, and contributed a great deal to his enjoyment of life.

The Oxford into which Henry Smith was now thrown had almost recovered from the strong ferment which ended in Newman's going over to the Church of Rome. The leaders of the High Church party had either followed their captain, like Christie and Bowles, or had satisfied themselves, like Mark Pattison, that

Protestantism does not admit of a divided allegiance. There were still High Church cliques among the undergraduates, such as Newman has sketched with caustic subtlety in *Loss and Gain*, which discussed Church matters from the Anglo-Catholic point of view, but they rarely got beyond a mild dilettanteism. Even this was not always treated with a proper tolerance. I remember a debating society of young Churchmen, which so irritated the Protestantism or the common sense of a rather sporting College by carrying a resolution that 'St. Augustine's interference with the British Church was uncatholic and uncalled for,' that at its next meeting the orators were dispersed by the agency of hot pepper thrown into the room, and saluted with a baptism little short of total immersion as they left the quad. Of the fast men of that day, it need only be said that they have been inimitably limned for good and bad in *Tom Brown at Oxford*. Outside these two sets, which have perhaps attracted more attention than they deserve, and also outside the common and obscure men, were the abler young men of the University, Conservative or Liberal in their politics, as temperament or training determined, but mostly with a wholesome share of English secularism, and neither High Church, except in rare instances, nor aggressively Protestant, nor to any appreciable extent Freethinkers. Lord Salisbury, Lord Kimberley, Lord Brabourne, Sir M. E. Grant Duff among politicians ; Goldwin Smith, Sellar, Grant, Sandars, Poste, and Conington among men of letters or scholars ; Spottiswoode and Rolleston among men of science ; Chitty among judges ; Sandford and Ducane among officials, were some of the Oxford men of Henry Smith's day, and with most of these he was more or less intimate at some time, while Grant Duff and Conington were among his dearest friends. Whatever time or thought men of this type could spare from work for the schools, was divided between politics and literature ; and Henry Smith's University letters are a singularly faithful reflex of the spirit of the period. They are more mature and temperate than perhaps any one but himself could have written, but they show the enthusiasm for intellectual eminence which is the salt of Oxford life ; and the admiration evinced for Mill, and the praise, however qualified, of Robert Chambers, are evidence that the writer was already to be numbered among the few on whom Carlyle had no hold.

Of Henry Smith's Oxford career it may briefly be noted that in 1848 he won the Ireland University Scholarship, the blue ribbon of classical scholars ; was a double first-class in the Lent Term of 1849 ; was elected Fellow of Balliol in

November 1849 ; and gained the Senior Mathematical Scholarship in 1851. He was unable through absence to stand for the Hertford Scholarship, which falls to the best Latin scholar of the year ; or for the Junior Mathematical ; and he was beaten for the Senior Mathematical Scholarship in 1850, the first time that he stood for it, by Mr. Ashpitel of Brasenose ; the single defeat of the kind, I believe, which Henry Smith sustained.

Balliol College, to which Henry Smith belonged, was far away the best in the University during the time of his residence, and for some years afterwards. A variety of circumstances had contributed to build up its pre-eminence. The first cause was the far-sighted integrity of the old Master, Dr. Jenkyns, who was almost singular among the Heads of his day in regarding it as the first duty of a College to promote intellectual distinction, and who waged an incessant war with privilege, abolishing gentlemen-commoners and throwing open close endowments as far as he legally could. Dr. Jenkyns could not have done much single-handed, but he gradually found or created men, often no doubt abler than himself, who were glad to carry on his work in the same spirit ; and the late Master of Balliol, Mr. Jowett, then one of the tutors, was undoubtedly the soul of the College during the whole time of Henry Smith's connection with it. At the time of Henry Smith's election, the College wanted a mathematical lecturer. There is no doubt, I think, that he was chosen in the well-warranted expectation that he would consent to reside and lecture. In this way began his own lifelong union with Oxford, for until then he had been a mere bird of passage. Having once decided to accept the office thrust upon him, he gave himself up heart and soul to doing his work well.

It was a common story in Oxford at that time that Henry Smith, being uncertain after he had taken his degree whether he should devote himself to classics or mathematics, had solved the doubt by tossing up a halfpenny. His sister remembers how he actually expressed a wish that some one would do this for him. He was, in fact, the last man on earth to have committed any important decisions to chance ; and he has himself told me that his choice was partly determined by the fact that having at that time weak sight he found he could do more work in thinking out problems than in any other way without using his eyes. The decisive reason was of course a pre-eminent genius for mathematics—the born aptitude that is itself fate—and the cause why the determination was made at that particular time may have been this offer of a lectureship. Nevertheless the Oxford tradition is so far valuable as it testifies to the general belief that Henry Smith could have made his mark in any study he embraced. 'I do not know,' Professor Conington once said to me, 'what Henry Smith may be at the subjects of which he professes to know something; but I never go to him about a matter of scholarship, in a line where he professes to know nothing, without learning more from him than I can get from any one else.' Once it seemed as if he would be attracted into chemistry. The College demanded of him that he should give chemical lectures (1853), and Henry Smith accordingly became a pupil under Professor Story-Maskelyne, who then occupied a laboratory under the Ashmolean Museum and gave instruction in chemical analysis. Here H. Smith showed that in delicate manipulation and in accuracy of work he possessed a sort of instinctive faculty. A lifelong friendship grew out of the hours spent in this way; although the demands of a new and engrossing science on his time were too great to permit his sacrificing to chemistry the many other important subjects and duties that filled up his life. Even then, however, I remember, his idea was to seek numerical relations connecting the atomic weights of the elements and some mathematical basis for their various properties*, so that we might anticipate experiments by the operations of the mind—an ambition which was very interesting to Alexander von Humboldt, when Sir M. E. (then Mr.) Grant Duff told him of it. Ultimately Henry Smith of course found that science is too jealous a mistress to admit of a divided allegiance; and, though his reading was always wide and various and singularly well digested, he practically devoted himself to mathematics, and as I understand to two or three great subjects with which his name will always be associated, the Theory of Numbers, the Theory of Elliptic Functions, and certain new processes of Geometry.

One point for which the generations younger than Henry Smith and John Conington will always remember them gratefully was the way in which they mingled in undergraduate society. The distinctions of academical rank were at that time rather jealously marked in Oxford. If the tutors and fellows were

---

* His conviction that such a numerical and mathematical basis underlay the phenomena of chemistry was even stronger in the case of crystals. At my suggestion he undertook the discussion of the principles involved in the parallelism of zone-axes and face-normals in a crystal system with rational indices; the results of which were given by him to the London Mathematical Society in vol. viii of its Proceedings.—N. S. M.

not, like the Heads of Colleges, in inaccessible isolation, they were scarcely better known to us through the formal breakfast parties which were submitted to on both sides as a very irksome duty. Here and there a man, like the admirable Charles Marriott of Oriel, made it a duty to invite young men, in order that they might feel at liberty to go to him if they needed religious advice, which was never obtruded ; but men of this stamp were never, as far as I remember, more than genial hosts. Henry Smith and Conington, men of the most opposite temperament though devoted to one another, threw themselves with such unaffected simplicity into our interests and occupations, that we all came to regard them as personal friends, and to talk as freely before them as before one another. Looking back I can see that their position was that of very helpful and sympathetic seniors at a children's party, and I can conceive how Smith's playful sense of fun and Conington's grave humour must often have been tried by the obligation to treat our criticisms of men and things or our forecasts of the future seriously. That the intercourse was begun and carried on on their part from a conscientious desire—due partly to Arnold's teaching—to convey a serious interest into everyday life, I at least cannot doubt. As one who profited by the association let me record that meetings of this kind were not only the most pleasurable part of a chequered Oxford life to many of us, but unquestionably did more to stimulate thought and form character than the more formal influences of the chapel and the lecture-room.

A letter from one of Henry Smith's old pupils, Professor Irving, of Melbourne, will complete the description of this part of his career, and speaks with authority on some matters which I only knew from report.

Melbourne,
1st September, 1888.

My dear Pearson,

It is by no means an easy task to carry back the memory nearly forty years, and recall scattered reminiscences of one from whom you have been altogether parted, with whom you have not even kept up communication by letter for more than thirty years.

Yet such in the old Oxford days was my affection for, and so highly have I ever honoured him whom I was then proud to call my friend, that I must accede to your request and do what little I can towards your presentment to the world of Henry Smith, Scholar and Mathematician.

My first introduction to him was, I think, in my Freshman's Term at Oxford, Michaelmas 1849, the term in which he gained his Fellowship at Balliol ; but our intimacy really dated from the beginning of 1850, when he became our Mathematical Tutor. From the first there had been this link between us, that I had inherited the little third-floor rooms in the inner quad of Balliol, which had belonged to Scholar Smith, as he was called in those days to distinguish him from sundry others of the same patronymic.

I remained his pupil in Mathematics throughout my undergraduate time, and was able to do him the credit of winning the Junior Mathematical University Scholarship in 1850. Of his power as a Class Teacher I cannot speak, as I was almost alone with him : but my individual experience was that as a Teacher he was all a learner could desire, most patient with all one's difficulties, most clear and full in his explanations. But he was too kind to me. He sympathized strongly with my disappointment when the authorities refused me permission to compete for the Ireland in the spring of 1850, and knowing how keen my desire was to win that distinction in the following years, he did not force me to work at Mathematics as I ought to have done, and so I failed to do justice to his teaching, and attain his own class in the Final Honour Schools.

Through Smith I made another valued friendship, that of John Conington, Professor of Latin, and might have gained access to the intellectual circle in which they moved, and of which they were such brilliant ornaments. But I must honestly confess that my own work for the Schools was sufficient mental exercise for me, and that I sought my relaxation, not in other spheres of thought, but on the river.

Yet in our frequent intercourse there was quite opportunity enough for me to learn and to appreciate the manysidedness of Henry Smith's mind. All of my generation were prepared to look up to and to admire one who had done so brilliantly as he had in Oxford : and when you came to know him personally you could not look upon that splendid forehead of his without assurance of the powerful intellect it betokened : you could not converse with him without realising that he was one of whom it might be said that 'omne scibile novit.' And what he knew, he knew, not as so much stored up learning to be brought forth as required, but he had made it all his own, he had thought as well as read.

Still with all his vast erudition, and his great intellectual power, he was the humblest, the gentlest of men. Ignorance, even if pretentious, was not to him something to be crushed with sledgehammer Johnsonian blows, but a thing to be pitied and kindly enlightened.

In fact were I asked to select his peculiar moral characteristic, I should say he was the most gracious man I ever knew.

Reading over these lines, I recognize with regret how very imperfectly are therein expressed the love and admiration I felt for him, how feebly they serve to set him forth.

Yet inadequate though they are, they may help somewhat. If I cannot do better—

       ' His saltem accumulem donis, et fungar inani
       Munere.'

      I am, my dear Pearson,

          Yours ever sincerely,

            M. H. IRVING.

In 1855 some of the abler Oxford and Cambridge men determined to publish
a yearly volume of Oxford and Cambridge Essays, and Oxford led the way, T. C.
Sandars, I believe, being the guiding spirit and editor. Henry Smith contributed
an essay on the Plurality of Worlds to this publication. He took for his theme
Whewell's then unacknowledged book on that subject, and Sir David Brewster's
fiery answer, ' More worlds than one, the Creed of the Philosopher and the Hope
of the Christian.' The subject was a fascinating one, and Henry Smith was in
many respects admirably calculated to do it justice. He wrote as simply and
clearly as Herschell or Tyndall, and he was skilful in dissecting arguments of
every kind with faultless impartiality, so as to reduce them to their absolute
value or no-value. A single passage will serve as an illustration of his method.
Whewell had argued in the spirit of Lucretius that there was, so to speak, a law
of waste traceable in the Divine economy, and supported this position by facts
from the origin of species. ' If we found,' Henry Smith remarks, ' that Jupiter's
four seasons differed so slightly from one another that they hardly deserved the
name, and that they could not be conceived to be of any use to his hypothetical
inhabitants, we should be reminded by those "rudimentary seasons" of the osteo-
logical facts on which the essayist dwells so much, of the rudimentary fingers in
the hoof of a horse, or the rudimentary paws with which a snake is said to be en-
dowed. But the one thing we should not be prepared to find would be a wasted,
imperfect, uninhabitable planet. We should know of no facts in Zoology with
which to compare such an occurrence. The crust of our earth is filled with the
remains of departed life, but we find not a vestige of imperfect attempts, of forms
moulded after the vertebrate type, and yet incapable of animation.' It will be
remembered that both essayist and critic wrote in the days before Darwin, and
that Henry Smith had never made any special study of comparative anatomy.
With this allowance it must, I think, be recognised that Whewell's conception
of a general law producing a single successful result and failing in every other
case was substantially and hopelessly wrong, and that his critic's conception of
' a law uniformly asserted in a multitude of individual cases, and uniformly pro-
ductive of variously perfect results,' was a singularly correct expression of all
that science was then able to teach.

There are passages of characteristic irony scattered through the essay.
We are told that in one of Plutarch's Dialogues, ' the lunar world is connected
with the future destiny of the human soul, after a manner which, we conceive,

Sir David Brewster would allow to be highly creditable for a heathen, and on the whole corroborative of his own opinion.' Of the literary form of Whewell's essay it is said : 'In the dialogue at the beginning of the essay the earlier letters of the alphabet, who appear as the objectors, conduct themselves so much like simpletons that one wonders at their being thought worthy of so long an interview with the enlightened Z.' Of theological arguments intruded into the domain of science it is observed : 'We cannot imagine a more painful spectacle of human presumption than that which would be afforded by a man who should sit down to arrange "in a satisfactory way" a scheme for the extension of Divine mercy to some distant planet, and who, when he found "great difficulty in conceiving" such an extension of the Divine attribute, instead of desisting from his vain attempt, should go a step further still, and infer that no such scheme can exist because he fails to discover a *modus operandi* for it.'

Still, though the article on the 'Plurality of Worlds' was read with pleasure and spoken of with esteem, its success was not so unquestionable as to tempt its author into larger literary work ; and his only other contributions of any length to English prose are, I believe, a review of Mr. Freeman's *Federal Government*, which he wrote for the *National Review* in 1864, and the Memoir of Professor Conington, which was prefixed to the volumes of his works in 1871, and which is a very perfect example of skill in recording a quiet life so as to invest it with interest.   It would have been a great misfortune for science if a man capable of enlarging its boundaries had wasted his powers upon mere criticism or exposition ; yet, considering Henry Smith's unambitious temperament, which made him careless of personal fame, and his invariable readiness to oblige friends, I cannot doubt that he might have been seduced into Quarterly Reviewing or some other form of ephemeral literature if he had possessed some of the minor qualifications of a journalist.   The fault of his argumentative writing is a disposition to hold the balance and to avoid summing up ; and it is in keeping with this quality that his style, though it has the subflavour of irony and the point inseparable from lucid concentration, is not epigrammatic or what would be called strong.   The writer's tenderness of disposition had something to do with this characteristic.   He who as a boy of fifteen had stopped himself in a caustic criticism in a private letter because the subject of it was 'somebody's bairn' carried the same thought for others into his words and dealings through

life. Reserve on matters that lay near the heart was another modifying influence.
To many men, the scholar who identified himself with every movement for religious
or intellectual or political freedom in the University was still more or less a
sphinx because he never propounded his convictions as a topic for conversation.
The world that reads is rather like the world that listens to a platform orator.
It likes its instructors to be positive, even where they cannot be certain, and to
have its conclusions presented to it in the form of short and simple aphorisms,
which it may swallow and retain without trouble. Henry Smith could not have
attained to this ideal, and it is matter of some satisfaction that he did not
aspire to it.

In 1857 Mrs. Smith died. The attachment of mother and son to one
another had been deeper than is common, and the course of their lives had
drawn them nearer together than can often be the case. It was now arranged
that Miss Smith should keep house with her brother in Oxford, the two
spending the term together, and each being allowed complete liberty of movement during the vacations. I cannot doubt that this arrangement contributed
very much to Henry Smith's happiness. He was eminently domestic and
hospitable, and having the cares of household life taken off his hands, and being
supplemented by one who was almost another self, was able to fill his house
with friends, who were certain of an Irish welcome, however unseasonably they
might arrive to ask for a dinner or a bed. He was also able under his own
roof to gratify his passion for pets—Persian cats of distinction and two aristo-
cratic dogs—to which there are frequent allusions in his letters. During the
vacations he often visited the Continent, going once to Sweden and Norway ;
more than once to North Italy ; to Spain with Grant Duff in 1864 ; and to
Greece in 1872 with Mr. and Mrs. Grant Duff. From time to time he paid
visits to an old friend of the family, Miss Theodora Price, who had lived with
his mother during the whole time of her widowhood, and who, on Mrs. Smith's
death, established herself at Tunbridge Wells. For some years, too, Henry
Smith was a prominent figure at the various meetings of the British Association
in England, Scotland and Ireland. It will be seen that his life was in no sense
that of a recluse ; and it may be added that he entered with zest into every
form of social enjoyment in Oxford, from croquet parties and picnics to dinners.
That the irregular, desultory life, with its frequent breaks, suited his health is
probable ; and, as he possessed a rare power of utilising stray hours so as never

to intermit work altogether, **even when his distractions were most numerous,** it seemed possible that **he might** be among the singular few who have combined residence **in an** English University with unswerving devotion **to the claims of** abstract research.

Fortune appeared to favour this anticipation. In 1860 Mr. Baden Powell, **the Savilian Professor of Geometry, died, and** Henry Smith **became a candidate for the vacant post.   Some years before, he had told a friend that to occupy this chair was the great ambition of his life.** He said that the two Savilian Professorships were the most honourable offices in the University : they were open to the whole world of Mathematicians, and had usually been held by distinguished men.   His wish was now to be gratified in the pleasantest way. Those who would naturally have been his rivals, the other Oxford mathematicians, were the first to draw **back in his favour and sign a common** testimonial to his pre-eminent claims*.   I well remember the generous warmth with which **two of the senior** professors, **Mr. Walker** and **Mr. Bartholomew Price, but** especially the latter, expressed themselves to me **at the time** about Smith's undoubted genius **and the chances** that he **would one day** leave **a name** to be remembered beside those **of Newton and Laplace.   The electors for the chair chose** him, as I have understood, without hesitation, taking the view that as no other Oxford man was a candidate, **and as** Henry Smith was pre-eminently qualified, it was needless **to scrutinise** the testimonials of outsiders.   He himself was a little troubled **by a doubt whether the claims of an older man, Dr. Boole, of Queen's College,** Cork, ought **not to have received further consideration.   That Henry Smith** justified his electors **by the magnificent work he did later on, is beyond question.**   He was also **a very** successful teacher, **having what must be considered large classes** in a University where mathematics have, at least in recent times, attracted comparatively few students.   Passages in his letters **prove how** keenly he

---

* I can express no opinion worth having on this subject ; but I see from **a notice in the** *Academy* (Feb. 17, 1883), written evidently by a personal friend, that much of **the work given to the world in** later years had been produced before he was thirty-five. 'He (Professor Smith) communicated at different times a good many notes and papers to the Mathematical Society, especially during his Presidency in 1874-76 ; and we believe that all the results he gave he had had in his possession for fifteen years.' His work on the Theory of Elliptic Functions and the Introduction to Professor Clifford's *Remains* belong however to the last seven years of his life.

promoted the well-doing of his pupils, and what his views were about the reforms desirable in mathematical teaching.

The present volumes show what splendid contributions Henry Smith made to science during the short twenty-nine years of his speculative activity. Nevertheless, it must, I think, be admitted that his unrivalled powers were often employed upon work that scores of able men might have been found to do efficiently, and which his friends should not have asked him nor he have consented to undertake. From 1850 to 1870 he was Lecturer at Balliol, not being able to afford to give up his Fellowship, and having scruples about retaining it if he did not teach, as the number of Fellowships was limited and the stipend of a Lecturer was too small by itself to remunerate any one for the work. It must be borne in mind that during part of this time he was also Savilian Professor, and during the whole of it he was constantly doing other College and University work*, assisting backward men, or taking part in examinations, or serving on University Boards and Committees. In 1873 he freed himself from the worst of this drudgery, the College Lectureship, by accepting a flattering and generous offer from Corpus Christi College of a Fellowship upon that foundation†. Not long afterwards he obtained the Keepership of the University Museum, left vacant by the death of Professor Phillips. The office gave him a pleasant house, a small stipend, and not very uncongenial duties, half as master, half as servant,

---

* The Master and Fellows of Balliol College, for instance, once asked him to give a course of lectures on the Schoolmen; and he complied.

† A friend at Balliol writes :—'We knew perhaps better than others how necessary this relief was to Henry Smith, and we rejoiced that it had come to him; we knew likewise the perfect loyalty towards his old College which prompted his resignation. Nevertheless, it was a grievous thing to us that he should be obliged to leave our body. Never had we felt so bitterly the difference between a poor foundation and a rich one. Henry Smith, as Steward of Common Room, was our chairman on social occasions, especially at our annual "gaudy" on St. Catharine's Day. The last speech he made in this capacity was immediately before his migration to Corpus. He assumed a playful tone, and tried to amuse us by various quaint comparisons into forgetting our loss, but he was quite unable to subdue his own emotion, and he was weeping himself before he had made us laugh. This was the only time that I ever knew him break down. Though ceasing to be a Fellow, he continued to give us the benefit of his presence and counsel at our College meetings. By the next St. Catharine's Day the keen and constant interest which he took in our affairs had somewhat reconciled us to the change, and this feeling was warmly expressed by the Master in proposing Henry Smith's health. I remember the Master's concluding words, which struck me at the time as a note of warning, and which have now a sadder significance : " I will only venture to express the hope that he will not suffer himself to be numbered among those men of varied powers and charming manners who have given up to society and business what was meant for science and posterity." '

which sate lightly upon one who was genial and full of instinctive tact. Nevertheless, it cannot be said that his work was sensibly lightened for any long time. Partly, he was himself to blame. He had a speculative element in his nature, and had invested so much money in mines—almost always, I am afraid, unremunerative—that it became important now and again to eke out his regular income. I remonstrated with him very strongly, when he added the duties of Mathematical Examiner at the University of London to his other heavy work (1870), for he seemed to be breaking down at the time he undertook it, and I felt sure that whatever he did for the day's need was so much taken from more enduring labours. It seemed however as if the world was in a conspiracy to force duties of every kind upon one whose talent was so flexible and whom men of all opinions agreed to welcome as a coadjutor. He was for years a member of the Royal Commission on Scientific Education, having been appointed in 1870, and he drafted a large portion of its report. In 1877 he became a member of the Oxford University Commission under Lord Salisbury's Act ; and in the same year he agreed to be chairman of the new Meteorological Office, the governing body of which was practically nominated by the Royal Society. This latter work was specially congenial, and the associates were so considerate and able as to give a charm to toil ; and Henry Smith enjoyed the fortnightly visit to London, and the temporary rest from the turmoil of Oxford business. Still, when all is said, it can hardly be doubted that the labours of all these various offices meant a partial interruption of nobler toil and may have hastened a premature death.

It may perhaps be said, and not without some truth, that those who knew of the condition of his health should have refrained from heaping work upon him and should even have compelled him to take a long term of real rest. But in fact these demands came on him from several and distinct quarters, and what might seem to each person or group of persons making the demand a light and congenial undertaking for the always gracious counsellor of 'golden speech,' became, when added to the aggregate of such undertakings, a serious, perhaps even a fatal burden. The truth is that his presence was always welcome on Boards and Committees ; for he possessed the rare gift of suggesting some middle course which would often effect an agreement between persons who had been advocating opposite points of view, and of so bringing about a welcome end to a weary discussion.

It will be a melancholy satisfaction to some of the friends with whom Henry Smith went on holiday expeditions, to reflect that these intervals of rest were not only periods of unmixed enjoyment to him, but probably helped to prolong his life. The letters he wrote from Greece in 1871 will not bear reproduction, but are full of the pleasure he experienced. 'We certainly had a most perfect voyage.' 'Except Pylos, I don't think we missed seeing anything we could have seen. Grant Duff, in a place he has not seen and wants to see, is quite perfect ; and we shall now work morning and night, till we have done Athens well.' 'All that is in Athens we have done to the greatest perfection,' is the comment in another letter. If only excursions of this kind could have been more frequent! The last I find commemorated is a visit to Rome in 1879, when Henry Smith represented the Meteorological Council at the International Meteorological Congress.

In 1878 Mr. Gathorne Hardy, who then represented the University of Oxford, was raised to the Peerage ; and the Oxford Liberals determined to bring forward Henry Smith for the vacant seat, in the hope that his great personal popularity and unrivalled academical reputation might win over many votes from moderate Conservatives. Moreover Henry Smith was not emphatically opposed to the Jingo or war policy of the Beaconsfield Ministry ; the test by which Conservatives especially weighed politicians in that particular year. He did not expect success, and he hardly desired it, but he would not shrink from a fight if he was asked to stand forward as the representative of a principle. I am told his friends were sanguine of success for a time. Friends are bound to be ; but no sane looker-on could have anticipated any other result than that which actually took place, that the Conservative candidate would be elected by an overwhelming majority. I have never felt that, in this particular instance, the rejection of an eminently good and wise man was unconditionally to be regretted. Personally, I have no sympathy with the doctrine that scholars are out of place in Parliament—a doctrine which would have excluded Macaulay, Gladstone, Cornewall Lewis, Goschen, Fawcett, Grant Duff, Morley, and Bryce among office-bearers of recognised ability, as well as Grote and Mill and a host of others who have added distinction to the House of Commons although they never attained to office. I am convinced that Henry Smith would have been as popular in the House of Commons as he was everywhere else, would always have been listened to when he spoke, and would have spoken with effect. Still I cannot persuade myself that his magnificent powers could have been adequately employed in debating or administering: and I am certain that dozens of inferior men would have played their part as usefully in St. Stephen's; while there was no one but himself in England so peculiarly fitted to increase knowledge in one very difficult and abstruse department of enquiry.

If however Henry Smith had ever gone into Parliament, he would have been something more than a representative of learning or even of academic Liberalism. He had a genuine sympathy with the poor of his own land; and his last public appearance anywhere was in the Oxford Town Hall to support a resolution by Mr. Arch in favour of giving the franchise to the agricultural labourer. The speech then delivered will bear reproduction for its own merits, and is a good specimen of the speaker's style; that of a man thinking aloud in simple words, yet with an instinctive perception of rhetorical effect.

Professor Henry Smith said it was as a Liberal that he would say a few words with reference to the resolution before them. In the course of his life he had found himself sometimes on the extreme left of the Liberal party, sometimes verging towards its right— for every party had a right and left—and pretty often about in the middle of it. He was bound to say that his belief was, in the first place, that the whole of the Liberal party, right, left, and middle, was unanimous in thinking that the National Agricultural Labourers' Union had rendered a great service to the United Kingdom. He further believed that the whole of the Liberal party rejoiced to think that the great benefit which that Union had conferred upon the agricultural labourers of this country would remain for ever associated with the name of Mr. Joseph Arch. He would endeavour to support the resolution by an argument different a little from those they had heard. The extension of the household franchise to the counties was inevitable; whether they liked it or not, it was a thing which must be done. He believed there were but few men in this country—sensible men, men who looked at what was around them, and who listened to what was said—but felt that it was inevitable. He was one of those who, when it was clear that a thing must be done, believed that the sooner it was done the better; and if it were for that reason only, he would heartily support the resolution. But, in addition to that, he did believe that the extension of the franchise to the great classes who now were excluded from it would, as had been well put before them already, exercise a beneficial influence upon the future course of their legislation. It might be true that some persons might ask what would the agricultural labourer and the rural artisan do with the franchise when they got it? They would do like other people. He feared they would do some mischief, for he knew no class of his countrymen among whom there were not some who did mischief with any right that was entrusted to them, but he firmly believed on the whole they would exercise the franchise for good. If he were told they would exercise the franchise for selfish objects, for objects peculiar to their own class, he would say let it be so; but if so, what would they say to the other classes who already possessed political powers? Could any one of them send a representative who could say that his hands were free from selfish legislation? If they must count—for, alas, they must—upon some strain of selfishness in their common nature, at least let them take care that their representation was not one-sided, but that at any rate each class had a fair means given it of defending itself from others. It was for these reasons that he for one most heartily supported the resolution. He hoped to see the household franchise extended as rapidly as possible to the counties, and he was not one of those who shrank from a still greater consequence which would come when that great measure of enfranchisement should be followed by an equally sweeping measure of redistribution of seats.

From that platform Henry Smith went home to die. Overwork and sedentary work had gradually undermined his constitution. When I last saw him in 1879 he still looked well, and in some respects, from having filled out a little, less delicate than as a young man, but I noticed that he was less capable of sustained effort. In 1881 premonitory signs of a break-up of the constitution showed themselves, and were unhappily not heeded as they should have been. First he suffered from his digestion, and had to put himself under Sir H. Thompson's care; and then a stoppage in one of the veins of his leg confined him for many months to the sofa, and made all but occasional carriage exercise impossible. He seemed to be tiding over this illness, when a rush of University work threw him back again into the condition of an invalid.

When he spoke at the Town Hall meeting he was suffering from a cold. The exposure and excitement were followed by congestion of the liver, which was the more dangerous after the severe attacks which had followed on the Roman fever, from which he suffered in 1845. On the morning of Thursday (February 8) there seemed to be a change for the better, but at noon the worst symptoms returned; and Sir William Gull, who had been telegraphed for and who arrived about eight o'clock, held out little hope. About four o'clock next morning (Friday, February 9, 1883), the patient's state was declared desperate, and three hours later he passed painlessly away.

He was buried (writes a friend who was present) at St. Sepulchre's Cemetery in Oxford on Tuesday, February 13. So great a concourse of undergraduates as well of senior members of the University and friends and strangers from a distance has rarely been seen on an occasion of the kind in an English

University. An academic funeral is always an impressive spectacle, and the long line of the procession and the scene in St. Paul's Church and around the grave in the cemetery will never be forgotten by those who were present.

For once there was no discordant criticism over a grave. Not only did all agree to speak with tenderness and admiration of the dead man, but there was a singular consent of opinion as to his character and pre-eminent intellect. The funeral procession that carried him to his resting-place was nearly a quarter of a mile in length, and included every man of position or note in Oxford and many others distinguished in their various ways who had come from every part of England to pay the last honours to a dead friend. The *Times* wrote of him as 'one of the most remarkable men of his day,' and the *Spectator* declared that 'it would be difficult among the world's celebrities to find one who in gifts and nature was his superior.' 'Some of us,' said Professor Stubbs (now Bishop of Oxford), in a University sermon, 'can remember the youth of brilliant promise, of almost unparalleled achievement in all our studies; all of us have before our eyes the manhood of indefatigable energy, of most generous devotion, of most kindly and effective sympathy with all good work; the entire expenditure of consummate accomplishments and of every bright gift on the work of Oxford.' Perhaps however no words were more frequently before men's eyes or in their thoughts in connection with Henry Smith's death, than a tribute which Sir M. E. Grant Duff had once paid him in the House of Commons, in commenting on his nomination as one of the Oxford University Commissioners. He said :—

'Professor Henry Smith is not merely in the first rank of European mathematicians, but he would be a man of very extraordinary attainments even if you could abstract from him the whole of his mathematical attainments. He was the most distinguished scholar of his day at Oxford. . . . But Professor Smith's extraordinary attainments are the least of his recommendations for the office of Commissioner. His chief recommendations for that office are the solidity of his judgment, his great experience of Oxford business, his services on the Science Commission, and his conciliatory character, which has made him perhaps the only man in Oxford who is without an enemy, sharp as are the contentions of that very divided seat of learning.'

To myself, who am no mathematician, and who therefore cannot estimate Henry Smith's intellectual power in the departments where it was highest, it has seemed also, as it seems to Sir M. E. Grant Duff, that I have never known his equal or perhaps one who could be classed with him. What always impressed me however was not so much his marvellous versatility or his thorough mastery of everything he touched, or his conversational brilliancy—though none of all these can be separated from my recollections of him—as his singularly clear judgment, combining insight into the essential truth of whatever he examined and balance in the summing up of it. Never did genius more completely take the form of sublimated common sense; and this effect was undoubtedly enhanced by his unassuming manner. What he had to say was never thrown into a doctrinaire form, half dogma, half epigram, but was stated in the simplest possible words. Sometimes no doubt an opinion given in this way would attract less attention than it deserved and it would certainly be less effective than a brilliant paradox. Gradually but surely those who met Henry Smith, or who came to him for counsel, perceived that his insight was unerring, and learnt to defer to his judgment, the less reluctantly as 'he had the great art of never pressing a victory home, and of bearing defeat with pleasant equanimity [*].' Perhaps it was this faculty of judgment which kept him from being over-weighted with his learning. He had read many books which even scholars rarely open, and he never forgot what he had once read. I remember for instance how he gave me on one occasion a most amusing account of the Letters of Synesius, which Kingsley's *Hypatia* had, I think, induced him to look up. His knowledge of Protestant Hymnology was curiously intimate and wide: and, when he assisted a friend to compile the University Hymn-book, his recitals from memory of whole hymns by Wesley and others impressed those who were present as very remarkable. Even his private friends, however, only learnt by rare glimpses what his acquirements were; and in general society, though he never affected to be other than a scholar, he impressed those who met him as a man of the world with perhaps unusual cultivation.

His friends sometimes compared him to Pascal, with whom he had many points of resemblance, the combination of mathematical and general ability, a keen wit, an extreme reserve, and an unfortunate lack of personal ambition. There was, however, one remarkable difference. Pascal, who has recorded the opinion, 'Diseur de bons mots mauvais caractère,' meaning, I suppose, that an epigram is a truth pared to a point and twisted into a barb, was yet seduced by his genius into endowing the world with a book that scathed and blasted the

---

[*] *Spectator*, Feb. 17, 1883.

cause and the men he assailed. Henry Smith's tenderness of feeling interfered with his command of literary form. He had a feminine instinct for avoiding whatever would give pain, and never allowed his buoyant spirits to betray him into a word that might seem harsh, or his inimitable persiflage to pass the boundary line into sarcasm. Those who heard him talk were conscious of wit that played round every subject with a perpetual sparkle, and that left a delicate aroma behind; but no one ever knew it employed as a weapon of offence. Reading over his private letters I find the same kindliness, the nearest approach to personal satire being perhaps the description of a heavy dinner, 'with four pièces de résistance, not including X and Z,' two rather overwhelming talkers. Therefore if Henry Smith had ever written on any of the subjects on which he felt strongly—and he was an ardent Liberal on every University question and on almost every political topic of interest—I cannot doubt that he would have adopted a style of earnest simplicity, and would have trusted for effect to argument, enhanced at most by a restrained eloquence. Bearing in mind that he was confessedly one of the most brilliant talkers of his day, so that every obituary notice dwelt lingeringly upon this trait, and considering how easily the playful but keen humour might have been transformed into caustic satire, I can only wonder at the mixture of kindliness with strong self-discipline that prevented even an occasional lapse. Both in this matter and in his judgments of men and things, a singularly fine character gave law to the intellect. He was clear and just in expression because he was accurate and truthful in thought; he was irreproachable in speech, because he never allowed himself to cherish an ill-natured thought.

Any one who has been often in the society of brilliant talkers can hardly have failed to notice how little of the best conversation is of a kind to bear record or is practically remembered. Dr. Johnson was singular in attracting an unrivalled biographer, who took notes unblushingly, and was skilful enough in literary form to polish up what he took; and Sydney Smith's fertility was so great that some of his mirth has survived him: but of George Selwyn and Luttrell, of Fox and Canning, of Macaulay and Bagehot, we know disappointingly little. Two or three trifling instances may serve to show what Henry Smith's manner was. He was once winding up a mathematical lecture by explaining a new solution of an old problem. 'It is the peculiar beauty of this method, gentlemen,' he concluded, 'and one which endears it to the really scientific

e

mind, that under no circumstances can it be of the smallest possible utility.'
He was obliged to pass through France in 1870, when fortune had just turned
against the French armies, and the cry of treachery was raised everywhere.
A guard noticed the tall Englishman with a blonde beard and spectacles, and
instantly denounced him as a German spy. A suspicious crowd collected in
a moment around the carriage. 'Gentlemen,' said Henry Smith with an
amused smile, 'I speak French very badly, but not I hope with a German
accent.' The proof and the speaker's impressive serenity carried conviction,
and the crowd melted away. 'You take tea in the morning,' was the remark
with which he once greeted a friend, 'If I did that I should be awake all day.'
A friend mentioned to him the enigmatical motto of Marischal College. 'They
say; what say they; let them say.' 'Ah,' said Henry Smith, 'it expresses
the three stages of an undergraduate's career. In his first year he is reverent,
and accepts everything he is told as inspired : "they say;" in his second year
he is sceptical and asks "what say they?" and "let them say" expresses the
contemptuous attitude of his third year.' At a time when English society
was perhaps extravagantly fluttered by Lord Beaconsfield's apparent success
at the Berlin Conference, Henry Smith reduced the event to something like
its proper proportions. 'Dizzy,' he said, 'has taken John Bull to Cremorne,
and the old gentleman is rather pleased to have been there.' On the news that
a distinguished friend, who was also markedly pessimist by temperament, had
been appointed to a high post in India : 'How fortunate!' was the remark ;
'it will give him another world to despair of.' He summed up X, a brilliant
writer but inconsecutive thinker, in the criticism, 'X is never right and never
wrong ; he is never to the point.'

It is sometimes said of loveable men, that they diffuse their affections
so evenly as to be incapable of strong personal attachments. With Henry
Smith to be a friend once was to be a friend for life. The masterly biographical
sketch which he wrote as an introduction to Conington's Miscellaneous Writings
will give a measure of one friendship that lasted from school days till it was
interrupted by death. Professor Rolleston, who could hardly ever speak of him
without some epithet such as 'the golden-mouthed,' confided his family when
he died to Henry Smith's care, and the trust was accepted and discharged
with exemplary fidelity. Probably no other great student was ever so ready
as he always was to put aside books and papers when a friend entered the house.

Yet his nature, genial and hospitable in the extreme, was not what is called an effusive one. He has noticed in the life of Professor Conington, that that great scholar, after he underwent a spiritual conversion, used to speak of his experiences unreservedly though in the simplest language. On this as on every subject of delicacy, Henry Smith was absolutely reticent. He would discuss religious topics if they were started as matter of interest, but I never knew him talk of his own faith, and I should be slow to believe that he ever did. My impression is that he accepted Christianity not only as a habit and a conviction, but as a rule of life, and in fact his character can scarcely be explained, except by ranking him with those who feel that they are ' ever in the great Taskmaster's eye.' I think he regarded much popular theology as irrational, and much fashionable doubt as a mere winnowing of chaff. Some of the weightiest words I ever heard from him were on religion. Beyond this I can say and surmise nothing, and his letters are not more unguarded than his speech was*.

The one question as to Henry Smith's character that appears to be still undecided is, whether his inaptitude for self-assertion, his scorn of personal ambition, his severe acceptance of duty in whatever shape it came to him, are to be regarded as blemishes or excellences. The distinguished friend who wrote about him in the *Spectator*† has shown in thoughtful and wise words how much there is admirable in the ' philosophic life '—' life of exemplary moderation, far removed from even a suspicion of worldliness and vanity.' ' Great moral gifts,' as the writer goes on to say, ' can be found when occasion demands them ; talents grow on every tree. But the serenity of heart which enables its possessor to wear the gifts of genius with sobriety, and to use them nobly and well, without seeking to expend them in the purchase of fame, or wealth, or of advancement, is a quality which modern society little cultivates and seldom sees.' It may seem to those who ponder this temperate and lofty apology, that it is a sufficient answer to the regrets I have freely expressed in this sketch over genius that was often lavish of itself on work for the moment's need or work of ordinary compass. Let me say for myself and for those who think with me, that we never desired wealth for Henry Smith except in such measure as might free him from sordid

---

* He on more than one occasion spoke to me on these subjects. His position was perhaps most simply expressed in a conversation in the course of which I remember his saying that the essential features of the Christianity held to-day were held in the time of Justin Martyr.—N. S. M.

† The article is printed at p. 50.

necessities, or fame except as a recognition of what he might achieve ; and that
the world's opinion or the state's honours could not have raised him in the
estimation of those to whom he was already above all men. Our feeling about
him was essentially what Newton expressed when he said that 'if Cotes had
lived, we should have known something.' It is very possible that those who
saw how much of his time Henry Smith gave to Examinations, and Boards, and
Commissions, and who unconsciously estimated the range of human effort by
their own measure, did injustice to the special capacity I have noted in him
for carrying on consecutive work in stray. moments. It has been said by one
who can speak with authority on such a subject that Henry Smith was ' the author
of mental achievements in the most abstract and complicated of the sciences,
which will rank as scarcely second to any in the century.' On this matter the
collected works will be conclusive evidence. What, however, surviving friends will
and must feel is that genius is as rigidly bound to husband its powers as mere
capacity, and that nothing can be spared from the supreme work of life without
loss *. Prove to us that Henry Smith's work was indeed scarcely second to any
in the century, and we are constrained to assume that, had his energies been more
severely economised, it must have been second to none. Certainly the ordering of
these things is not in our hands. He who gave the perfect intellect gave also
the fine temperament, the tenderness that shrank from disobliging, the modesty
that esteemed no duty undignified, the absolute disregard of self. To us who
knew him, let me repeat, the man was always greater than any possible work he
might do, though we set no limits to its possibilities ; and to us the ever-green
wound of his loss is partially compensated by the remembrance of . an ideal
character. What we grieve for is that generations that did not know him
as we have known him will try him by the only standard possible, that of
his completed work, and will give him less than the measure of his real
capacity, though they can never refuse to number him among the great names
of the century.

---

* I may add, however, to this that, frequently as I urged on H. Smith to turn a deaf ear to some of
the too many supplicants for his time, and to give up some of his less important occupations, his answer
to me always was that he did ' get all that he could out of himself' as it was ; that in truth his greatest
work could only be done now and then, and could not be reeled off the mind indefinitely. Much
interval was necessary to him.—N. S. M.

EARLY LETTERS.

To HIS SISTER.
                                            RUGBY,
                                    Sunday, Sept. 18, 1841.

I wrote you a letter about a fortnight ago, but as I had no direction, I did not know where to send it, and so I have it still. I had a great mind to send it just as it was to you, although the news would certainly be rather stale. And, I must say, I think it would have served you right. The most important piece of information I have for you is that there is one more girl in the world than there was when I last wrote. In other words Mrs. Highton has a daughter, by this time two and a half days old. The baby is a very healthy one, and Mrs. Highton is doing very well. Mr. Highton told me to-day that he used never to be able to tell one baby from another, but that he thought he should be able now. This reminds me that he was not able to understand a passage in Lucretius, describing the raptures of a lover, till after his marriage. In fact his capabilities of comprehension are decidedly on the increase. Young Alfred Highton, (who by-the-bye is uncle Alfred) has entered the school and is vastly improved to my mind of the matter. I had to set two long punishments to two of Price's fellows the other day, for which I have incurred great hatred from some of that tribe. Owing to this ill-feeling, when I entered the school the other day I was greeted with a loud hiss. Now Mr. Cotton, wisely 'considering that the offence against one was totally merged in the general offence against the masters, thought it best that they should keep it in their own hands.' This saved me the trouble of thrashing —— myself, though it was worse for him personally; for Cotton ejected him from the 5th, and Tait added a flogging, and he sprained his own wrist, so he has been altogether unlucky. But no more of this, for although —— is as great a blackguard as you could wish to see, 'he is somebody's bairn.' How long do you mean to stay in the land of potatoes, alias the Emerald Isle? Write soon to

                                    Your affectionate brother,
                                            H. J. S. S.

To HIS MOTHER.
                                    RUGBY, *May 1842.*

You must expect only a short letter from me as I am in a great hurry. I should have written to you before but for my having had so much to do. I have heard from Ellen a day or two since, and I find that I have a letter which I wrote to her, I do not know how long since, lying to this day in my drawer. I think I have given both her and Charles reason to be very angry with me. I have only written to the latter twice and that was quite at the beginning of the half. But as for you and Miss Price I have treated you both most admirably, at any rate compared with my conduct last half.

Tuesday is the Queen's birthday, and a whole holiday. I have been [asked] to Mr. Dicey's, but have declined going, as I am very much behindhand in my work for the examination, which begins in a day or two; I have been too 'cute to tell this to Mr. Highton, or he would almost oblige me to go, and I should not tell you but that it is too late for you to write to tell me to change my decision, if you were so inclined. I am **beginning to** look forward to the **holidays**. They begin Friday fortnight. I know I shall **be heartily** glad when they **do** come, for besides the pleasure of seeing you and all the rest, I am heartily **tired of** the school work.

I really know of nothing else to tell you, everything goes on as it has done, except that there has been a slight row in the way of a fight with the town. I fully expected several fellows would have been sent away, but the Doctor has thought differently, for he went round to all the Forms and told us he was very glad to find the school not in fault. This is my only time for walking in the week, and it has just set in raining which has almost made me weep.

Your very affectionate son,

H. J. S. S.

————————

To his Sister.   London,

Wednesday Evening, November, 1844,

You will be sorry to hear that another delay has intervened to defer the time of my leaving England. Saturday is now the earliest day on which I can hope to embark at **Folkestone.** Cartwright*, who took no notice of the note I sent him from Oxford, **can give me** not another moment's time till eight on Friday morning, and the steamers **leave both** Folkestone and Dover at 6·30 A.M. I have expended the sum of ·£4 12s. 6d. **on my clothes, and on books** £6 3s. 6d. The reason for which disparity is that I do care **for the one and do not** care for the other. Indeed I intend that Mr. Jowett, the tutor of Balliol, should bear half the blame that attaches to the last item, although I know that ultimately all the expense will fall on Mama.

In the Examination my two best papers were my English Essay and Latin Verses. If you wish to construe this favourably you will infer that my argumentative and imaginative faculties have been developed in due proportion. Yet in the latter I did not far recede from my own prediction. At Luzern, you know, I used to write five verses per hour. At Rugby I so far improved as to write six, or six and a half in a very urgent case. In the hall of Balliol my good genius inspired me with eight in each hour; in all twenty-four. If

---

* A famous dentist of that time in Little Burlington Street.

you add to these two old ones (they were all that would come in) you will have the number that I could write or did send up.   I suppose that not one of the better sort of candidates, I mean of those against whom I really had to contend, sent up fewer than forty-five.   Fortunately for me however length is a thing they care not for.   For my English Essay I willingly disclaim all originality, and return thanks with all my heart to the very few pages of M. Guizot that I read, I forget where, and to Stanley's life of the Doctor.   The subject was the connection of National character and different forms of Government. You (I mean yourself Ellen, who think meanly of my calligraphic skill) will feel an inward exultation when I tell you that in the private confab I had with Jowett he told me that both he himself and all the Examiners could not but notice the exceeding slovenliness (it is his own word) which disfigured the writing of all my papers, and I must confess that blots were there and erasures innumerable.   All the candidates (Grant and myself included) were floored, or nearly so, in the *vivâ voce*, to which Jowett made a somewhat sarcastic allusion when he advised me to give Homer and Virgil a prominent place in my studies.   My own Greek translations too (I mean my Greek verse and prose) were noticed as extremely indifferent, to which two papers, I think, another remark of Jowett's alluded, when he told me that my Greek scholarship was thought deficient ; at least so I would fain persuade myself ; and so I think was indeed the case ; for otherwise I should never have obtained the first place of all, which you must know mine was, for they gave my name out first ; then they said that they had found great difficulty in deciding who should have the second, and had [at] last decided in favour of Grant.   They gave my name out as formerly of Rugby School, which was exactly what I had wished.   In the preceding history you may evidently trace the consequences of the want of my Donnegan ; for it made me read much more Latin than Greek, and I think it will continue to be the case still, for at Rome I shall hardly care to invert the proportions of time I bestow upon each.   This is not an easy nor a short stage, but it is indeed down-hill work to speak of one-self.   Good night.

To THE SAME.   FOLKESTONE,
                                     Saturday morning.

At present I am detained at Folkestone because they would not call me in the morning. My portmanteau is gone to Boulogne, so are my new books in a separate brown-paper parcel.   The first is sure to be safe, but if the books should be lost you will never see me without tears all winter.   The six doctors have at last broken silence concerning Ward. They have summoned him into their awful presence (only think into the presence of Big Ben), and asked him, first, whether he acknowledged the work as his ? and, secondly, whether he acknowledged the tenets contained in certain extracts from it which they read to him. After deliberation for two days, Ward gave answer that he would do neither.   This seemed to puzzle the learned Judges of heresy and discourses of all truth.   Meanwhile Ward has published a species of abridgment of his work, and likewise a new edition of the whole in two volumes instead of one. Of course the refusal to acknowledge his authorship implies no denial of it, and is not intended to do so. It is simply a way to bogle the Dons. The Bishop of Exeter has issued a circular letter requiring every clergyman in his Diocese to wear the surplice in preaching. This of course contains within itself all the essential idolatry and will worship of Popery. For my own part I should not care if I were to behold the Comasarni cothurnus, or stockings as you call them, on one of our own Bishops, and I think the Bishop of Exeter ought to be made to wear them for his foolery's sake. It would be exactly such an infliction as he deserves. The offertory is the cause of another dispute, and of one the more violent inasmuch as Mammon mingles himself undisguisedly with the opposing party. Three to one on the Evangelicals and Mammon. And yet I wish the weekly collections were instituted if it were only that the Poor Laws might be over-thrown. They should not however leave the distribution to the clergy alone. Good bye, till Paris, but I fear I shall not have money enough to get much further, but I shall tell you more on the other end. Good-bye.   .   .   .

To the Same.   Oxford,
                                          Nov. 2, 1847.

I was very much pleased indeed when I found your present lying on my table this morning. I am really very glad you could not find a copy of Milton's Prose Works, for I would far sooner have the Political Economy, and moreover should have less excuse in getting it for myself.

I had to conclude my last letter in great haste, and yet I contrived to be late for evening Chapel nevertheless, so that I might have given myself more time.

.   .   .   .

The Bishop of Oxford preached yesterday at St. Mary's. I cannot say I was particularly pleased with him. He had a hard cause to plead for, the Church Missionary Society is not at home in Oxford, and I thought he was too much afraid of giving offence by over-praise. He has a wonderful way of adapting himself to his hearers, and yesterday he spoke of Saints and Baptism and Regeneration in a style so purely Oxonian that one could not help feeling it was ad captandum. Yet it was his way of saying things, rather than the things he said, that seemed meant to please ourselves and over done, and con-sequently he did not quite succeed; his Rhetoric was Anglican (that is an old Oxford phrase), and his Logic evangelical. Besides, a Bishop with lawn sleeves and a blue ribbon and a good deal of Court favour should not speak of life as 'a sandy and desolate waste,' nor compel one to think of his Hampden letters by reminding us that all Saints are 'very weak and very apt to err.' Still less should he make use of his father's memory to fill up a pair of round periods with 'one to whom the Eternal had committed the clientship of tortured Africa,' for 'history must tell aloud what filial reverence would more willingly contemplate in silence,' except that I have, spoiled his antitheses. However, it is not a very profitable employment this of dissecting a Prelate, even if he be somewhat too subtle an orator, so I shall let him go.

.   .   .   .   .

To the Same.

Since I last wrote to you I have seen a pair of litterary (this is the **correct spelling**, and besides displays the etymological connection with 'litter') stars, **though I confess of a** low magnitude. One is Froude (Shadows of Clouds man) and the other Kingsly, **if so** be I have written his name aright, author of a play called 'A Saint's Tragedy,' which you may have heard of. Froude is the more brilliant star of the two, and has more conversational power than any man I have ever seen, but withal contrives to persuade **you that there** is not an Opinion or Doctrine in this world he cares for. He will argue **against himself for argument's sake.** Kingsly (who is a Cantab, a country parson, and **a radical) looks on him with great** admiration and with approval nearly complete. He calls him **'an Angel Mephistopheles.'** On the whole, during the last week before Lent, I heard more **Radicalism than I have ever done in** my life before. I **suppose it was** all stirred **up by the** Revolution in France. At **a meeting of the Decad held in** Kingsly's honour, **a** motion in favour of a re-division of landed property **was carried by a** majority of 12 to 4. Clough (a Fellow and Tutor of Oriel) spoke for it, and moreover very well. He is by far **the most** far-gone **Radical** I see up here, but I like him, for he believes all he says (which is more than many people do) and holds his opinions very gravely. Of all Arnold's men he is most like him in character, but he goes far beyond **him in theology (so at least** they say) as well as in politics. I am very sorry to say they will not make him **head of a** godless College in Ireland. He would have done a great deal of good there : **in a godless** Society his theological opinions could not have done harm, and his learning, **his** liberal-mindedness, and his love of work would have been very useful : not that he would have regenerated Ireland.

Stanley and Jowett are **working away at a commentary on** St. Paul's Epistles, **but I know** not how soon it will come **out.**

To the Same.

I suppose that, like us, you had an eclipse of the moon last night and a mixture of April sun and April rain or hail to-day. Our eclipse came off very well : the moon was very nearly quite free from clouds when the eclipse was at its height, and beautifully clear towards eleven.

Newman has put forward a work. It is a novel like his sister's, but I have not found time to read it. It does not seem to be thought quite worthy of him, but it may be for all that.

Rugby **has** certainly been doing but poorly for some time : that is, so far as the scholarships are concerned, for in the schools we have as yet done very well. We have

just had a sufficiently mortifying defeat at University, where three or four Rugby men
were standing and yet were none of them elected. I suppose the University Scholarships
rank about third after Balliol and Trinity. If we do not get one of the Trinity ones next
term, we shall have let a whole year pass, a thing as yet, I think, quite unheard of.
I (and I may say the same for my fellow-scholars) am now fairly training for the Ireland.
We do nothing but compositions, or at least very little beside. For my part I have quite
given up Mathematics for the present, and Jowett, I suppose because he finds me apt,
seems inclined to work me well at least he tells me I ought to learn fifty or an hundred
lines every day by heart. This would be a very trifling matter if it were to be all verse,
but to learn fifty lines of prose every day would soon grow a hard task, unless one allowed
oneself to forget what had been already learnt. W. did more work at the beginning of term,
gave up the world, and took to reading; but whist and society are again getting a hold
upon him, so that unless he looks to it he will mar his chance for the Ireland.

To the Same.
Oxford,

March, 1849.

I have not read Froude's Nemesis. I have not had time. Nevertheless extracts from
it have been read to me, and, I think, I nearly know all that he has written in it. You
will find a review of it in last Saturday's *Spectator*, which I think exceedingly temperate and fair: only you plainly feel the writer's convictions on questions of religion
were not so decided as to tempt him to intemperateness or unfairness. The Nemesis
has been badly attacked in the *Morning Herald*. The first article was copied into the
Standard. Froude saw it there and wrote a reply which the *Standard* published, and
the *Morning Herald* of last Saturday contains its reply to Froude's reply. It is very
passionately written. I do not defend Froude's opinions, but his conduct with respect to
his College and his University (so far as I know the circumstances of the case) I am
prepared to defend to the uttermost, as I would Newman's. I think this sentence worthy
of coming from under a wig. The truth is that (to-day) I feel a partisan in the case,
having spent a great deal of last evening in a disputation against Goldwin Smith (whom
I then met, as well as I remember, for the first time). I certainly discovered a deep
pugnacity of which I before was wholly unconscious, for I am generally willing to purchase peace at any price. 'Nemesis' is the power of vengeance, divine wrath personified
by calling his book the Nemesis of Faith, Froude probably means that it is intended
to show how Faith abandoned avenges herself upon the Infidel: when his religion is gone
his whole moral nature becomes a wreck too. Thus you see the outline of the story
is sufficiently orthodox, but the impression that the book makes is derived from particular
parts. There is no immorality in the book (using the word in its technical sense), there is
a great deal of infidelity: it is beautifully written and with surpassing power. If you feel
inclined to read it after this statement I will try and find a copy.

To the Same.

Oxford,
April, 1849.

It seems that at last you are likely to come into possession of my real character. I think it necessary to make a few observations upon it to prevent all unfair conclusions. The points that I think successfully given are—Love of Approbation, which he has marked 20, Cautiousness 21 (it is my king organ), I think also I have a right to Conscientiousness, 20: and he has done decidedly well in marking Wonder below Ideality and Wit. I think too I have Order. His mistakes, in my own opinion (and if I am not likely to be impartial I am at any rate likely to know), are numerous. It is true. I have more adhesiveness than concentrativeness, but I have no right to so high a mark for it. I think I have more love of Life and perhaps more secretiveness than he gives me credit for. I certainly have more combativeness than destructiveness, but I am not sure that he is right in marking it 19. What is perfectly ridiculous is that while nearly all my known and observing faculties are marked 18, he should have marked Number only 16. Time he did well to mark below par. Altogether I do not think I am as slow an affair as I seem upon paper. You will easily see that 18 is his average, though he calls it rather large. My head apparently is of the average size*: I fall back upon this point continually : it is a great consolation.

I do not exactly know why you think I am in a worry about my reading. I suppose I must have employed some rhetorical phrases in my note to Mama. I have now taken a cold if that will give you any satisfaction, but I do not find that (as yet) it has had any depressing effect upon my spirits. I rather wish I could get into a fright with respect to the schools, for it is high time I should. As it is, I only awake at distant intervals to a consciousness that I am going into the schools unprepared, [I suppose all men write in this way to their sisters during the last three months but I am not sure] and then I yawn, and think that after all chance has a great deal to do with it, and then I metaphorically go to sleep again. Except my composition I do not feel safe in any one point, and though I can do a good deal in two months, I cannot do everything that I have to do.

A new book, entitled 'The Nemesis of Faith,' has been written by Froude and publicly burned by Sewell†. Froude has resigned his Fellowship, probably because if he had not resigned it, they would have endeavoured to expel him. I am not sure that they

---

* This result was confirmed by some measurements Professor Rolleston took afterwards. The proportions of the head were singularly fine.

† In justice to Mr. Sewell's memory, it may be said that the story, as I heard it not long afterwards at Exeter, falls short of a deliberate *auto da fé*. Mr. Sewell, I believe, found the book lying about in the Hall, which was used as his Lecture-room, asked if any one claimed it, and when no response was given, put it into the fire, with the observation that that was the only fit place for it. Mr. Sewell was a prominent man in Oxford and even in England for some years, as a writer of books mostly of a religious character (Christian Ethics, Christian Politics, etc.), and as the founder of two religious schools, St. Columba in Ireland, and Radley near Oxford.—[C. H. P.]

would have succeeded. He is going to Hobart Town, and **is to** be Principal of a new
Gower Street Institution out there. Conington tells **him**, he can burn Sewell's Christian
Ethics, or his Agamemnon, or his Essays on Plato, as soon as he has fairly set up his own
Educational Academy,—and thus requite Sewell for **his cruelty.** Froude ought really to
leave Oxford, for this blessed University is no sphere **for him**: it harms and is harmed.
Once fairly escaped from our peculiar holy water, or milk and water, I daresay he will do
very well. Frank Newman is now a friend of his., **He once showed** me a pair **of** notes,
one from F. and a **second** from J. Newman. The **hand-writings were** curiously **similar,**
only Frank's looked as if it were written with a good pen, while J. Newman's was **untidy.**

To THE SAME.   OXFORD,
                                        April 24, 1849.

Balliol has met since I last wrote, and the world, as well as **I can** see it through
my windows and in my daily walks, appears to be going on very nearly as it
usually does. . . . B. has come up and is **at a loss to** know what to do; he cannot
make up his mind **to take orders, not that** he sports scruples, for I do not think he does,
though it is the **fashion now-a-days, and though if a scruple were once** to possess itself of
his mind, it would **be hard to expel it.** But he is not sure that he is made **for it, and**
meantime I think he is **successful in attracting pupils to his rooms, so that I daresay** he
will do very well. Some of his friends appear to think he would make an excellent
bagman, but as this would not give sufficient scope for the religious element of his character,
I venture to propose a colporteur instead.

I perceive that James Bloomfield Rush has ended his mortal career. The *Times*
appears to have thought his last scene likely to impress men with an opinion of his inno-
cence, for their leading article was plainly intended as an antidote. I hate that paper.
I find reading for the Schools is decidedly bad for the temper: I find my capacity for
disliking opinions, persons, and principles goes on crescendo, so that I do not know what
I shall come to at last. Besides I am not always on the right side. I attribute the mischief to the thirty-nine articles, which one has to learn by heart and **say** like a cockatoo.
If ever I get a bird of the parrot species, I will teach it portions of these formularies: it is
possible for a parrot they might have some meaning. Except for the anathemas **at the**
end, I unhesitatingly prefer the articles of the Trent Council wherever I have compared
them, though by the way that has not been in every case. The article on original sin
would be blasphemous if it were not (most fortunately) nonsense: that on works before
justification is probably only nonsense. Predestination is a successful attempt at saying
zero in many words. 'Sunt et illi anathematizandi' is ludicrously absurd. However
I do not want to think of the articles any more than I need, and as I shall put on a Civil
Law gown, my signing them will be perfectly optional.

P.S.—I am amused at my own indignation against the articles: it is probably owing
to my having learnt twenty on Sunday and forgotten them on Monday.

To the Same.

OXFORD,
May, 1849.

The Examination is begun, that is to say it is nearly half over, and as I have been out walking my hands are so cold they will not hold my pen. The papers succeed one another thus: Logic, Latin Prose, Ethics, Greek Prose, History, Latin Translations, Essay, Greek Translations, Taste Paper. The Latin and Greek Prose I suppose I ought to have done, but I did it ill. I did not know much about the questions in Logic and Ethics, but then I did not expect to know much about them, so I was not disappointed. I expect to be plucked, for I have not looked at the Old Testament History for I know not how long. It will be by no means an unmingled vexation, for I shall have time to read between this and October. Moreover if I am not plucked I shall be floored, so that 'tis only a choice between evils. I am I believe the third man on Monday; 'numero Deus impare gaudet,' so that at any rate it is a good omen. I write better than this in the Schools. Good-night.

H. J. S. S.

Expect to hear on Tuesday that I am plucked.

To the Same.

OXFORD,
June, 1849.

I enclose a Class List, for I remember you expressed a desire to have one.

. . . .

I do not think there is anything more to say. It is 3 o'clock and towards this hour I begin to grow sleepy.

Most affectionately yours,
HENRY J. S. SMITH.

P.S.—I have got a series of outer garments and have received the cordial congratulations of Mr. Williams, who compared me to Gladstone, a friend and patron of his as he said. I shall endeavour to make it generally known that Mr. G. employs a dissenting tailor. It would be a *coup de grace* to his hopes of re-election. . . I have got an alpaca coat, which I could as soon fly in as walk in here, but it will do for Spa.

To the Same.

OXFORD UNION SOCIETY,
All Hallows' Eve, 1849.

. . . .

I am glad you are reading Ruskin; he is as full of prejudices as he can be, and he is too Anglo-Catholic, and I daresay he may have many faults beside. But I have never read a more eloquent writer nor one of more profound feeling. He is just married to

f 3

a Scot, and the Oxford story is that he fell in love with her while he was at school in Scotland. I have only read his second volume and that very cursorily, and as his style is not a nineteenth-century one, it really required time to understand him.

The 'New Timon' I have often heard of and have often seen and often heard quoted, but as yet I have not read a line of it, and very likely never shall. A lady is rarely seen in a Rugby study, and I should not wonder if my ghost would have occasioned less surprise than my sister to its present occupant. Mr. V. B. is about to produce a volume * of poems, partly his own and partly Clough's. Besides, Clough is going to appear before the world in a small volume of his own, but what it is to contain we do not know as yet †.

As for the 'Vestiges of Creation,' my conjecture was not only grounded on external evidence, but I heard it was his or read so I know not where. I think you allude to his notion that sight is a Photographic process, the retina being affected by rays of light exactly like a photographic plate. Moreover he is of opinion that all intellectual operations are necessarily attended by, even if they do not consist in, a similar photographic process. This is not a common opinion, and it is put prominently forward in R. C.'s ‡ publication as well as in 'Creation.' There are many things beside; the amount of belief in phrenology and the importance assigned to it is exactly equivalent in R. C. and in 'Creation.' But I depended more than anything upon the great similarity between their general conceptions of the whole of Nature, the perfect materialism of each, and the ways they resolve all phenomena of mind into phenomena of matter, the exact equivalence of their philosophic characters, shewn in their equal aptitude for premature generalisation. But I confess I never thought R. C. capable of writing a work like 'Creation' till I persuaded myself he had written it: as a work of art it is magnificent, and I think it would be pedantic to expect great accuracy of detail from a work like it.

To the Same.

OXFORD, 1850.

Albeit this letter is addressed to yourself, I would pray that it may be read aloud and listened to with attention, as it contains one announcement of importance, and very few of my letters can say so much for themselves.

In primis, I have taken a lodging for next term; it is almost exactly opposite to Balliol, in fact the distance from Hall and Chapel is hardly double that of my present rooms from the same places. I am to pay 20s. a week, which I may perhaps find inconveniently high, but which is not dear for the goodness of the rooms and of the situation. My landlady's name is Mrs. Bowell. I implore you do not pronounce it as if it rhymed with 'vowel,' though I am afraid it is the common pronunciation of the name in Balliol.

---

* This little volume was called Ambarvalia.
† This was the Bothie of Tober-na-Vuolich.
‡ R. C. Robert Chambers was, as Henry Smith divined, the author of 'Vestiges of Creation.'

They were the only rooms in Broad Street that I could find, and I was resolved not to go out of it.

Secondly, the mathematical lectureship has been offered to me by the Master, and I have accepted it, i.e. in case his present intention should continue till next term. I confess I was taken completely by surprise by this announcement. I suppose I had attributed more wisdom to the Master and the Dons than they can claim. This is an ungracious way of speaking of persons from whom I have just received so very flattering a mark of good-will and respect (I can really call it nothing else), but all I have to say is they prefer having work ill done by an in-college man to having it well done by an out-college one, and this I think is not wise. I could only say that I felt myself quite incompetent, and I don't remember that I ever spoke with a clearer conscience. But as he did not think proper to consider my testimony against myself decisive, I had to answer that I should be guided entirely by his wishes. He then told me that I was to consider the matter as settled, and so I suppose it is.

Now the conclusion to be drawn from all this is very plain. I cannot spend my Long Vacation in total quiescence, if this is the proper phrase. I have in fact promised to do as much as I can during the Vacation to fit myself for the sudden transition from learner to teacher. Accordingly I must do some work. I have not the faintest intention to over-read myself, and do not mean to begin at all for some time to come. But I hold myself bound to get through a great deal of mathematical reading during a part—say two months—of the Vacation. My work as Lecturer will be exceedingly light. I am not to take the elementary classes, so that I shall not have to read with more than eight or ten men. But if I do not prepare myself beforehand, I shall not only do my work very imperfectly but also I shall really have more to do. In a word, my Long must have more books and fewer wanderings. Switzerland, I think, ought to be given up, at least so far as a walking party is concerned. If you think it well for me to try Wiesbaden, we can easily do it, but I should not like to be in a perpetual state of locomotion. . .

Ever yours,

H. J. S. SMITH.

To THE SAME.

Oxford,
Feb. 26, 1852.

After Carnival comes Lent, and with it a respite from incessant dining out, which enables my thoughts (sweet creatures) once more to turn homewards and to visit you all in your spacious apartment as you sit cowering round a vile stove, vainly regretting English fires, English carpets, English sofas, English cleanliness, English society, English books, English honesty, English cookery, English mutton, et cætera. I should imagine you must all be very tired of Brussels; how very stupid it must be, and how dull you must all feel. I would not stay there even to get married, which all my friends seem to consider the *summum bonum* upon earth, the final cause of terrestrial existence, the be-all and the end-all here. X. desires to marry some one spirituelle. Z. is not at all particular and would marry any one that would marry him.

I hope you like the new Administration. I am glad that Disraeli is to lead in the Commons; it would have been a shame to put any one else over him, not to say that it would have been difficult. As you see the *Times* you probably know as much about it as I do or perhaps more. I never do more than glance at the papers, and frequently trust to hearsay. . . . It quite weighs on my spirits to think how dismal you must find Brussels. Miss B. must be the only star on your horizon how your affections must twine round her.

Last Thursday night from 9 till 1 we had such an Aurora Borealis as you can hardly imagine (it would have made even Brussels for a moment interesting). At 11¾ it had formed itself into a mass of crimson light directly overhead, which seemed to be fed by streams of vapoury light, which converged to it from all parts of the northern horizon, and which looked at times substantial and sometimes spread over the whole sky as a kind of luminous mist.

RECOLLECTIONS OF PROFESSOR SMITH.

I. BY PROFESSOR JOWETT*.

MY recollections of Professor H. J. S. Smith extend over about 40 years. I first heard his name mentioned in the year 1843, by the late Archbishop of Canterbury, then recently elected Head Master of Rugby, who told me that there was a boy in the School quite deserving of a place by the side of Conington and Walrond, who were the great names of Rugby in those days. He was going to try for the Balliol Scholarship. At the end of the year, on that occasion, he beat all the other candidates, of whom one was the late Sir Alexander Grant, elected Scholar at the same time with him. I remember him in the *viva voce* part of the examination, a youth of eighteen, rather overgrown and stiff, as youths of eighteen are apt to be, construing Latin and Greek authors in a pious and evangelical tone of voice, which provoked a smile in the Examiners, but with never-failing accuracy. The old Master, as we used to call him, took up his English Essay and showed it to me, saying, in his emphatic way, 'There's mind in that.' The subject given for Latin Hexameters at that examination was the Pelasgi, of whom he did not forget to mention in his verses that 'they worshipped nameless gods.' Meeting Arthur Stanley on the Woodstock Road the day after the election, he congratulated me on our having chosen a youth whose fame had preceded him at Oxford.

He more than justified the promise which he had given. Though not a poet or creative genius, he was, I think, possessed of greater natural abilities than any one else whom I have known at Oxford. He had the clearest and most lucid mind, and a natural experience of the world and of human character hardly ever to be found in one so young. He took up all subjects at the right end; he knew whereabouts the truth lay even when he was imperfectly ac-quainted with the facts. And he was the most amiable and good-natured of

---

* Professor Jowett's death has deprived these 'Recollections' of the author's final revision.

young men. I might apply to him the words in which Plato describes the youthful Athenian Mathematician, Theætetus, where he says : 'In all my acquaintance, which is very large, I never knew any one who was his equal in natural gifts. He had a quickness of apprehension which was almost unrivalled, and he was exceedingly gentle. There was a union of qualities in him which I have never seen in any other, and should scarcely have thought possible, for quick wits have generally quick tempers . . . but he moved surely and smoothly and successfully in the paths of knowledge and enquiry. He flowed on silently like a river of oil. At his age it was wonderful. He was also surprisingly liberal about money, though his fortune was only moderate' (Theætetus, 144).

The facility with which the youthful Scholar of Balliol picked up all sorts of knowledge was equally wonderful. During the first two years after his election to the Scholarship he was struck down by a serious and almost fatal illness, and did not come up to Oxford until what is usually the third year of residence had commenced. In the interval, residing in Italy he acquired a considerable knowledge of Roman inscriptions and antiquities, and also of modern languages. Within the year and a half which remained of his Undergraduate course he obtained the Ireland Classical Scholarship, and a double first. Two years later, the Senior Mathematical Scholarship was awarded to him. Similar honours have only been gained by one other person—the late Very Rev. G. H. S. Johnson, Dean of Wells, an eminent man, but little known, who, from ill-health, was unable to do justice to his great natural talents.

After he had taken his degree, he at one time thought of going to the Bar, for which he was very well suited—he would have risen rapidly to the high places of the profession. But the feebleness of his constitution when a young man led him to abandon this intention, and he soon settled down in the post of Mathematical Lecturer at Balliol College. The other tutors were the late Rev. E. C. Woollcombe, Dr. Lake, the present Dean of Durham, and myself. The Bishop of London (Temple) who preceded him in the office had just left us. In those days he was almost equally a lover of Classics and Mathematics. There was a time when he was quite divided in his allegiance between them, and used to say, in his free and easy way, that he 'must toss up a shilling to decide.' Even in the last years of his life he was in the habit of taking with him Greek books to read during the Vacation. In conversation he left the impression of being a well-read scholar, and a real critic, who was never led away by ingenious conjectures or uncertain fancies. For some time he was intending to edit the Timæus of Plato for the Clarendon Press, but he never had leisure to carry out this project. He finally determined, and probably he was right, to make Mathematics the chief work of his life.

The Mathematician is more cut off by his pursuits from his fellow-men than the student of any other branch of knowledge. He has interests which are locked up in his own breast, pleasures and also pains which he cannot communicate to others; the better part of him is moving about in a world of numbers and figures which have no connection with ordinary life (cp. Plato, Theætetus, 184 D). His study is apt to become a passion with him and affects his character. I am sure that this was true of Professor Henry Smith. It was the smaller part of him which we knew or could appreciate. His mathematical speculations could have been shared by a very few, not more than two or three, of his contemporaries at Oxford. Yet he did not withdraw himself from business or society. He was not the silent philosopher who is lost in reverie, or who, while acknowledged to be a mathematical genius, is pointed at by mankind as a poor and eccentric mortal. He was a thorough man of the world and greatly liked by everybody. He was very manly in his bearing, and quite free from shyness and nervousness in any company. He had a kind greeting for servants, and felt a real kindness for them—they were devoted to him. His manner of behaviour towards all sorts and conditions of men might be described as exhibiting a singular 'urbanity.' He was decidedly good-looking, and there was a certain intellectual distinction in his features and expression. It is necessary to combine these various aspects of him if we would duly estimate him. He was everywhere, and known to everyone, the life and soul of a social gathering. But he was also a thorough student, and an omnivorous reader, passing several hours of the day in abstruse Mathematics, but nevertheless acquainted with all new books, and on a level with every recent scientific enquiry.

He went on teaching at Balliol College as Mathematical Tutor for about thirteen years; at the end of that time he was appointed Professor of Geometry: he then combined the duties of Tutor and Professor. While only a Tutor of Balliol he had hardly any pupils worthy of him. The College, having at that time no Mathematical Scholarships, had seldom any good Mathematical students (those who were being usually men who read for double honours). His duties were, for the most part, confined to the preparing and examining men for Responsions. But he never thought it beneath him to take pains with any one, and he was an admirable teacher. He used to have his pupils on a Sunday afternoon to be examined by him, and would tell them that 'it was lawful on the Sabbath Day to pull an ass out of the ditch.' The better men were of opinion that they learned more from him in a few minutes than from another in a whole hour. He was constitutionally apt to be late and irregular in lecture, and on occasions of business as well as at a dinner party was often the last to arrive, but every one was very willing to wait for him. The circumstances of the University hardly admitted of his raising up a School of Mathematical pupils, but he was the life and centre of the study while he was with us.

He was very desirous to promote the interests of Natural Science in Oxford, and was in favour of some measure which would have made the knowledge of a portion of some one of the Natural Sciences the condition of obtaining a degree. The teachers of these sciences had long been fighting a battle against the older traditions of the University; they had now become the study of a few, but he clearly saw that they could never truly flourish until an interest in them was more generally diffused and they had a congenial atmosphere. But he was also the best friend that the older studies then had in the University, for he could speak with authority, and he was firmly convinced that in education Science should not supersede Literature. He deplored equally the want of literary culture which he observed in many scientific men, and the gross ignorance of the most general facts of Science which prevails in the world at large, especially at English Universities and Public Schools. In a similar spirit he was anxious to encourage at Oxford the study of Medicine and also of Engineering, thinking that they would supply a missing link between the Physical Sciences and the older studies of the University.

A considerable portion of his time was devoted to College and University business. Though he transferred his name to C. C. C. about ten years before his death and nominally ceased to be a member of Balliol College, he continued to show the same earnest interest in its concerns which he had always done. He took the same part in its Examinations and College Meetings—the only difference being that he no longer received the stipend of a Fellowship from it. There was never any one more affectionately regarded by the Fellows, or whose opinion had greater weight with them. He had the art not only of doing business well, but of making it pleasant, often with a slight jest or play of words smoothing away difficulties. I do not remember his ever having had a quarrel or difference with any one in the University. It will be easily understood that such a man was well adapted to keep men together and to carry things forward. At the Hebdomadal Council, where he usually appeared rather late in the day, he gave life and animation to every discussion. He seemed to say things in a better way than anybody else, and in an argument there was no one who was a match for him. When a new measure had been put into form by the Council he was very often selected to carry it through Convocation, his popularity and his manner of speaking having great weight in that assembly ; and it was whispered that 'the Council relied for the success of their measures too much upon Henry Smith's oratory.' Though well aware that the order and discipline of the University must be maintained, he was always a very earnest supporter of freedom, and a great enemy to the imposition of useless restrictions upon Undergraduates. He was indulgent to the failings of young men, and felt a humane pity for persons who had lost their character. He was one of whom it might be said that 'he would have stood by a friend, not only in adversity, but in disgrace.' Two occasions on which he distinguished himself were long remembered by those who heard him,—once in the Common Room, more than thirty years ago, when some of the elder members of the College sought to impose a new-fangled test upon the undergraduates instead of the time-honoured Thirty-Nine Articles. He pleaded earnestly for the retention of the latter, alleging that 'old chains were smoother and easier to the wearer of them.' The other occasion was in Congregation, about twelve years ago [1880], when he introduced a measure granting privileges to Colonial Universities, and drew a sketch of the growth of the London University, and of the mistaken policy of Oxford and Cambridge in their opposition to it.

He was not an orator, but a very good speaker, who had the faculty of thinking when on his legs, never faltering for a word, able to strike out, right and left, good-humoured and telling blows. His speeches were clear and luminous, and they also had the merit of keeping up the attention. Above all, he had tact. He said what he ought to have said, and abstained from giving needless offence. As a writer, he never attained to considerable eminence. He was the author, when quite a young man, of a very clever review in the Oxford Essays of Sir David Brewster's 'More Worlds than One.' In this paper the fallibility, both of men of science and of theologians, was impartially exposed, and I remember that Bishop Temple remarked, after reading it, that 'the author could do many things well, but that he would write better than he did anything else.' The prophecy was not destined to be fulfilled. His mind was drawn in another direction, and he had not the poetical gifts which seem to be indispensable in a great writer, whether of poetry or prose.

He was wanting in initiative. Though a very able supporter of the plans of others, he rarely, if ever, took the first step in introducing a measure himself. He was easy-going, not burnt up with a fiery zeal for change, but satisfied in

g

general with the world as it is, and really, I think, somewhat deficient in practical originality. He was contented to be a follower rather than a leader in most of our University contests. When he was brought forward a few years ago, rather against his will, as a Candidate for the representation of the University in Parliament, he was, I believe, absolutely indifferent to the result. I never knew a man, possessing so much ability, with so little ambition. Hence he interfered with no one, and as no suspicions were entertained of him, everybody was willing to do justice to his great merits. Nor had he any sympathy with new opinions in politics or theology. In politics he would have professed himself a Liberal, but he was not an advanced one. He was willing to talk about them, and his views were always worth hearing, because they were not strained out of newspapers, but the result of his own reflections. He was an acute political economist, a disciple of Mill and Ricardo, not much interested in the wider field which is sometimes claimed for the science. Nor was he at all disposed to undervalue the influence of theology. He was well acquainted with the results of German criticism on the Scriptures, but they seemed to make no difference to him. When he first came up to the University he was an Evangelical, and, for a while, retained his old belief. Indeed, some years after, on the occasion of a high-church sermon at St. Mary's, he would say, with indignation, 'that was not the sort of religion in which he had been brought up.' But, in time, the old clothes of his youth naturally fell off—he had out-grown them, and there remained a blameless character, a singular kindness and generosity, a love of justice and fairness, and a sense of religion which was wrapped in impenetrable silence—it was one of the subjects of which he least desired to talk.

He was very reserved. Like many other persons who pour themselves out freely in conversation, there was the appearance of *abandon*, but there were many subjects about which he rarely, if ever, spoke. One of these was himself. He was probably the confidant of many, for no man could give better advice in a difficulty, or was more willing to assist others. There was a feeling that he could be absolutely trusted, and even if a foolish thing were said to him, that he would not repeat it. His insight into human character was said, by one of his friends, to be 'terrible,' but it was never used by him except for some kind purpose. He could see through the vanity and folly of a friend, and yet retain a neverchanging affection for him. Of his own life, he seldom or never spoke ; he was not an egotist, and his own sayings or doings did not seem to interest him afterwards.

It is difficult to give an idea of his conversation. It was gay rather than serious, full of life and chaff, arising naturally out of the circumstances of the hour. If a stranger had come across him in a railway train, or had been his companion on a voyage, he would probably have found that this unknown person was one of the most agreeable men he had ever met. It was a great pleasure to have a tête-à-tête with him, for he was not one of those who required a company in which to show off. I have often decoyed him into my room for the sake of having a chat with him, and when once there, he was very willing to stay, for he was one of those who like to have a talk out and did not hurry away when the clock struck. In society he was ready to talk to every one, and every one was ready to talk to him. He had the art of setting people at their ease. He would at times break out into fits of laughter and joviality, which showed that the original Irish nature was not extinguished, but only kept under by him. Stories were repeated of his performances at Meetings of the British Association, which must greatly have enlivened that sedate assembly. He was certainly a wit, but his good sayings were of too delicate a fibre to be transplanted. To use Boswell's expression, his *bons mots* 'would not carry.' But they were the delight and admiration of those who heard them at the time. They possessed also one of the highest qualities of wit and humour, spontaneity. They were made on the spur of the moment with reference to something which was said or done at the time. And this very quality tended to impair their effect on those who were not present when they were first uttered, and did not know the occasion which had given rise to them. A light irony seemed to be always playing about his mind. It was the form under which he inclined to regard all human things, for he was very unimpassioned. An old school-friend would sometimes be the target at which he aimed. The great scholar, Professor Conington, a man so unlike himself, that their mutual friends wondered what could be the tie which united them, was often the butt of his humour. But the slight humiliation to which he was subjected was more than made up to him by the constancy and faithful attachment of his friend, who afterwards collected his literary remains and wrote his life. He was a little provoking to some others, especially to those who were too earnest or of too pushing a temper. He knew how, in Aristotle's language, 'to overcome seriousness by laughter,' or in other words, to make such persons appear slightly ridiculous. An enthusiastic friend might have thought him deficient in sympathy, but he was really always kind and considerate.

I hardly venture to repeat some of his good sayings, lest, detached from their surroundings, they should seem not to justify the high opinion which has been expressed of his conversational gifts. They are not of course of the quality of the best sayings of Charles Lamb or Sydney Smith, yet they are such as might have been said by them. The reader is requested to bear in mind their impromptu or occasional character. He who made them could have made many such every day of his life, and never aspired to be a wit, but only to amuse himself and his companions. At any rate they may serve to remind his friends of pleasant hours which they passed with him, never to return.

A friend told him of a rather ponderous jest made by Sir George Lewis, who, when Minister of War, once proclaimed in the House of Commons in a loud voice that he had ordered experiments to be tried respecting the comparative effect of 'short and long bores.' To this heavy piece of artillery Henry Smith instantly replied by asking whether he was not aware that 'smooth bores' were the most deadly of all.—Another friend said to him : ' What a wonderful man Ruskin is, but he has a bee in his bonnet.' 'Yes,' replied Henry Smith, 'a whole hive of them ; but how pleasant it is to hear the humming !'—The Lectures of a certain College Tutor were reported to be 'cut and dried.' 'Yes,' said Henry Smith, 'dried by the Tutor and cut by the men.'—A dispute arose at an Oxford dinner-table as to the comparative prestige of Bishops and Judges. The argument, as might be expected at a party of Laymen, went in favour of the latter. ' No,' said Henry Smith ; 'for a Judge can only say, "Hang you," but a Bishop can say, "D—n you."'—The next is of a higher class of wit. Speaking of an eminent scientific man to whom he gave considerable praise, he said : 'Yet he sometimes forgets that he is only the editor and not the author of Nature.'

The two remaining ones are autobiographical. He once said to a friend : ' C., I was kept in bed by illness when quite young for six weeks ; I then began to study mathematics, and I wish I had remained there ever since.'—Speaking to a newly elected Fellow of a College, he advised him, in the low whisper which we all remember, to write a little and to save a little, adding: 'I have done neither.'

These slight jests may perhaps be thought disappointing : it is probable that they are marred in the telling. They were the bubbles which were always rising to the surface of his mind, and though but poorly reported, may help to give to those who did not know him personally a faint idea of the charm of his character and conversation.

Though not rich, he was extremely liberal. He never seemed to think either about gaining or spending. He used to say that not enough money was to be had in Oxford to make it worth while to take trouble about it. Yet a certain love of speculation which was latent in his nature once led him into an unfortunate venture, from which he extricated himself by taking the affairs of a Company into his own hands, and at a considerable loss. For his services as a College Tutor he received a very moderate remuneration, but, having enough for his wants, he never seemed to desire that it should be increased. He did not wish to impose on the College a burden which it could ill afford to bear.

I have endeavoured, in a few pages, to give a sketch of one with whom I was in daily intercourse during thirty-five years of his life, and who I think may be regarded, without exaggeration, as one of the most remarkable persons of his time. Yet he lived and died almost unknown to the world at large. I have sometimes asked myself what was the reason of this contrast between his reputation and his real merits. It has been said that 'the world knows nothing of its greatest men,' but this familiar line, whether true or not, is not the whole account of the matter in his case. The explanation is partly to be sought in his own character. He had no ambition, he had not a strong will, and he had never made himself known to the public. He was once reproached by a friend for 'giving up to society what was meant for mankind,' and the reproof, as far as it applied to his life at Oxford, was not without foundation. He was not the author of any considerable work. His Mathematical writings, on which his fame chiefly rests, await the judgment of time. Though he managed, in great part, the affairs, not only of the University, but of several other great institutions such as Winchester and Rugby Schools, University College, Bristol, the University Commission, the Meteorological Office, the Oxford Museum, of which he was Keeper, and the Ashmolean Society, of which he was the Secretary, he could hardly be said to have left his mark upon any of them, however valuable his services have been to those institutions. To understand his superiority over his contemporaries, it was necessary to have lived with him and known him, to have heard him lecture, to have been with him at a College Meeting, to have enjoyed his society at a dinner-party, or on an excursion of pleasure. He never offended you, never disappointed you, he was never tired or out of humour. His greatness was shown in the peaceful continuity of a private life, not in great actions, or on striking occasions.

B. JOWETT.

II. RECOLLECTIONS BY LORD BOWEN *.

GREAT statesmen, successful generals, famous authors, distinguished men of science, eminent theologians—all those who have been raised by industry, talent, or the caprice of fortune, to prominence in a profession—become by degrees actors on whose movements our attention rests, and whose familiar figures are part of the spectacle of life. The public they have interested during their time bids them, when they die, a kindly and sympathetic farewell, retraces their career, counts up their successes, and assesses their general apparent value. Professor Henry Smith, whose loss this week casts a shadow both over Oxford and through many circles of educated men and women, belonged to none of these categories. To by far the greater number of Englishmen, his name is probably unknown. Some will vaguely recollect it as that of a candidate put forward unsuccessfully a few years ago by Oxford Liberals for the representation of the University. Many even of those who are aware that a man in the fulness of his powers is just dead, whose brilliant intellectual attainments have probably not been surpassed by any other of their English contemporaries, may, nevertheless, be surprised at regret so widely felt and so loudly expressed over the loss of one who wrote no great books, patented no great invention, amassed no fortune, made no famous speeches, and led no conspicuous movement, political or social. Measured by the popular measure of publicity and fame, Professor Henry Smith would hardly seem, to most of us, to have been one of the great men of the time. Yet it would be difficult among the world's celebrities to find one who in gifts and nature was his superior. Generally speaking, there is a rough justice in the sentence passed upon intellectual men who achieve no definite worldly success. We surmise, and often with truth, that some weak spot somewhere in their powers has been the cause of their failure to acquire those sublunary distinctions and rewards which coarser and more practical people manage to secure. To the case of Professor Smith, this kind of criticism would be inapplicable, for he possessed both the qualities and the character which might have made him famous in many active walks of life. His mental attainments were of the highest order. A finished classical

---

* [Reprinted (by permission) from *The Spectator*, Feb. 17, 1883.]

scholar, a mathematician, in some respects of European distinction, a considerable metaphysician, a trained master of most branches of knowledge, literary, economic, and scientific, an adequate linguist, and a man of sound judgment, perfect temper, and wise aptitude for affairs, he combined with his other special excellences a delicate gaiety of spirit, a brilliant conversational power, which made him one of the most accomplished and attractive ornaments of any educated company in which he moved. To what eminence in public or professional life accomplishments so varied might not have led him, it is difficult to feel sure, if only he had ever plunged into the stream of competition or adventure. But some delicate touch of indifference to worldly success mingled itself with his genius, and he remained to the last content with playing, and with playing well, whatever part fortune brought to him to play. Incessantly occupied in the discharge of duties both of a public and a private kind, that thickened round him as years went by, he was satisfied with what had fallen to his share in the lottery of life, and neither solicited nor ostentatiously avoided anything beyond. The 'note' of personal ambition seemed absent from his composition. And so it happens that the great public which takes its knowledge of men from newspapers and books, from debates in Parliament and the records of our Law Courts, hardly knew—if, indeed, it knew at all—Professor Henry Smith.

As the personal 'note' was wanting in Smith, so, on the other hand, the intellectual or academic 'note' was one which he possessed in, perhaps, its most attractive form. Vanity and self-seeking, every form of mental intemperance and extravagance, seemed to have no place in anything that he ever said or did. The last, the rarest triumph of education, is when it destroys the desire of self-assertion in a man of genius, and substitutes in its place the crowning flower of perfect moderation and equanimity. The greatest of Greek philosophers, in the greatest of moral treatises, has elaborated a theory that virtue consists in a golden mean, and in the avoidance of dangerous extremes ; but when driven into a corner for a standard by which the mean is to be measured, the illustrious moralist has no better compass to furnish for our guidance than this,—that the golden mean in each case must be that which is defined by the reason of some thoroughly temperate man. The result of Henry Smith's genius and culture combined seemed to make him the very man required by a philosopher for his human measuring-rod. A University life sometimes spoils and sometimes perfects natural capacities, but it usually leaves its mark upon them, whether it be for good or evil. Nobody could doubt but that Henry Smith, as he issued from the Academic mould, was a natural genius, with an impress of his University stamped distinctly upon him ; and Oxford has, perhaps, never had a more happy specimen to produce of her best influence than the late Savilian Professor of Geometry.

Smith came from Rugby to the University as a remarkable boy, and won the blue ribbon in all the great intellectual competitions of his undergraduate days. He became in due course a Fellow of Balliol, and joined a Common Room which consisted of a small group of very distinguished men. The present* Master of Balliol was already conspicuous in the society of Balliol Fellows, as the most successful and most energetic tutor of the first of the Oxford Colleges of the period. Among the rest were names of academic fame—Mr. Lake, the present Dean of Durham ; Riddell, an accomplished hero even among Shrewsbury scholars, whose beautiful character and refinement of mind were prematurely lost to the University by an early death ; Archdeacon Palmer, not the least distinguished of a trio of brothers with all of whom Oxford had reason to be content ; Lonsdale, Wall, Woollcombe, Walrond, and a few years later, Newman and Green. These were the days when Oxford, always passing through some phase or other, was entering on a new situation. The Tractarian movement had subsided, but the University was not at rest. A reforming Parliamentary Commission was troubling the waters. The old system of close Scholarships and Fellowships was slowly giving way, and like the rotten boroughs of a past political period, the close preserves of the Colleges were being either extinguished, or thrown open to public competition. But Oxford was still Conservative at heart. Leaders of the old school and their followers held the University pulpits, dominated Congregation, monopolized the best preferments, resisted to the best of their powers all local change, and were ready on provocation to ostracize unorthodox reformers for being, like Socrates, the corrupters of youth. Married Fellows were as yet unknown ; it had not yet become necessary to build whole suburbs of semi-detached villas to receive the feminine colonists of the future. But there was a stir and an agitation throughout the Academic world which the sense of changes, present and to come, had produced. University politics and polemics were, as always, of absorbing interest. Mansel and Goldwin Smith tilted against each other in debate before an admiring and competent academic audience. Oxford was, in fact, at war,—a war, it is true, polite, polished, and courteous.

---

* The late Professor Jowett.

Into this atmosphere, charged as it was with considerable personal electricity, Henry Smith was thenceforward absorbed; for nearly thirty years, no more attractive, brilliant, or genial figure was to be found in the perturbed society of the University. Some happy combination of judgment and temper made him acceptable even to those with whose opinions he had nothing in common. He succeeded in being a politician, without wearing the obnoxious colours of a partisan. He had the great art of never pressing a victory home, and of bearing defeat with pleasant equanimity. His business powers, his modesty, his wisdom, and his entire freedom from egotism and dogmatic presumption, a delicate gaiety that never flagged, wit that sparkled without wounding, and which rose incessantly to real brilliancy, made him not merely an effective personage in the Oxford world, but universally acceptable in any society, whatever the shade of its opinions. His finished persiflage, his pleasant epigrams, will long be remembered, though the brightest conversation is often the most evanescent, and the finesse of wit, like a musical laugh, disappears with the occasion, and cannot be reproduced upon paper or in print. As by degrees his attainments were recognized, both in England and abroad, his influence at Oxford naturally deepened; but neither within nor without the University did he grasp at opportunities for notoriety. Such power and authority as he possessed he held without an effort, without solicitation, apparently without any personal satisfaction in them. In offices of friendship he was constant; in such public or civic duties as came in his way, assiduous; no good or benevolent work ever needed a helping hand, but his was at its service, without ostentation, and without any expectation of personal advantage. He was a good speaker, without being a rhetorician; his death, indeed, last week was hastened by a chill caught or increased while he was addressing a gathering of agricultural labourers.

A life like Henry Smith's, of exemplary moderation, far removed from even a suspicion of worldliness and vanity, is seldom found in these days in combination with intellectual powers and practical ability on so considerable a scale. There are, no doubt, many nooks and corners in which at times may be seen flowering 'the wise indifference of the wise.' Students, divines, men of science or of letters, not seldom seem content to retire from the world, as if they had measured the true value of the things we most of us eagerly compete for, and were perfectly satisfied, of deliberate choice, to remain spectators of the fever of mankind. Some physical inaptitude, or some constitutional tendency, not unfrequently lies at the bottom of this apparently philosophic temper. Patient self-possession, and a sober estimate of the world and of

h

what it can give, are rarely found in a man who lives in constant contact with other men and their affairs, who shares in the interests of his generation, occupies himself with its business, and whose genius seems to bring high honour and success almost within his reach. Professor Henry Smith was not buried away from his fellow-creatures in literature, or study, or contemplation; he was no recluse or invalid, but a man of the world, active, competent, social, *only*—not ambitious. Personal serenity of such a type is rather a classical than a modern virtue; perhaps an age different to our own may yet regard it as one of the highest forms, not merely of intellectual, but of civic excellence. It is the characteristic of recent civilization, that in almost all its aspects it seems based upon a theory of personal competition. The prominent figures on every stage are the result of a struggle, not for existence, but for success. It is a contest which all seem satisfied to recognize as one of the conditions of ordinary life; which constitutes the essence of our politics, of our commerce, of our political economy, of our laws of property themselves. In the general race to possess more than the average share of wealth, power, fame, it is, perhaps, a wholesome lesson to turn for a short breathing-time to the uneventful example of the life of a man of genius, who was fitted for most distinctions, if he had cared to seek them; but who was unaffected by the universal fever, possessed his soul in perfect patience, and remained to the last content to discharge all the duties which Providence allotted to him, without affectation, and with that composure of soul to which great gifts are not always allied. The secret of the philosophic temperament, exhibited in this its most manly shape, is one which is not easy to explore; but when the phenomenon is seen, its charm attracts us the more in proportion to its rarity. Essayists and moralists for the last two thousand years have preached it, and inculcated it; some have gone so far as to boast of its acquisition,—its praise, certainly, is among all the prophets. Probably it is the product neither of Nature, nor of education singly, but of a happy, and of an admirable combination of the two. Among the many friends, acquaintances, admirers, whose thoughts have in the last few days been saddened or sobered by the unexpected death of a brilliant man of genius, there are none who will not readily accord to Professor Henry Smith the tribute of unaffected respect for what without extravagance may be termed his extraordinary powers of mind, his gentle and Laelian wisdom, and the sweetness of character which never made an enemy, lost a friend, or sought a personal advantage for itself. But besides this and beyond this, it may not be out of place, before a personality in many ways so complete fades into indistinctness, and a life ceases to be familiar to us which must hereafter be treasured rather in the memory of his contemporaries and friends than in the history of his time, to recognize in the Professor Oxford has lost that special type of wholesome and of manly virtue the growth of which is not much favoured by the rush and turmoil of these times. Great mental gifts can be found, when occasion demands them; talents grow on every tree. But the serenity of heart which enables its possessor to wear the gifts of genius with sobriety, and to use them nobly and well, without seeking to expend them in the purchase of fame, or wealth, or of advancement, is a quality which modern society little cultivates, and seldom sees.

III. RECOLLECTIONS BY MR. J. L. STRACHAN-DAVIDSON.

THE death of Henry Smith will be felt as the greatest loss which could have befallen Oxford. In him the University possessed a student whose knowledge and genius were honoured throughout Europe. Of those amongst whom he lived few indeed could follow him to the height of his scientific speculations. Most of us did not know enough to understand where and how he was working in the field of Mathematical Science. By us he is lamented as the wisest counsellor of the University, and as the delightful companion who gave life and charm to its society. Though his activity extended far beyond the limits of the University, he was very constant to Oxford. Since he took his degree he did not miss a single Term's residence. Re-elected time after time to the Hebdomadal Council, his assistance was called for whenever any serious business required sound judgment or delicate handling. His advice was generally followed, and if not, the neglect of it was almost always regretted in the sequel.

In Henry Smith were united to a rare degree knowledge of business and knowledge of men. He seemed most thoroughly in his element when swaying and guiding his fellows. To every matter which he took in hand, he seemed to come with a fresh mind, throwing off all the multitude of concerns which beset him, and unburdened by care or anxiety. Then under the cover of his easy playful manner it would soon become manifest that he had grasped all the true points at issue, and was ready with a firm and wise decision. He always looked facts in the face, and strove hard to distinguish the difficult from the impossible. To the more ardent spirits among his followers it was sometimes a matter of disappointment that he would not lead them to assaults which he saw to be fruitless. Though he could fight hard when the moment for fighting came, no one was more averse to multiply occasions of controversy. He saw things without passion and without prejudice, and laboured quietly and steadily for all that could advance the studies and promote the efficiency of the University.

In this spirit he accepted the thankless task of serving on the University Commission. It is the inevitable fate of such a body that their work is attacked at once by the criticisms of those who think that it has gone too far, and of those who would have had it go further. Henry Smith knew well that it was impossible to satisfy either the one party or the other. But it was a source of keen satisfaction to him to notice that when those who joined in complaining of the Commission came to propose alternative schemes they found that these divided them more than that to which they had objected. In the same way he was much gratified that it was only a minute point in the Commissioners' arrangements which was finally contested by the University. He claimed, and with justice, that when the Proctorial appointment of Examiners was the only portion of the old constitution which was defended to the last, it was pretty clear that the more important changes were acknowledged to be wise and necessary.

It may be interesting to note what Henry Smith thought of these greater changes. He fully appreciated the charms of the old system of celibate Fellowships, and never for a moment cherished the illusion that the new seven years' tenure could ever have the value and dignity of the old. But he felt that the old system could be practically worked only so long as the majority of Fellows were willing to take Orders and retire to a College Living in middle life. When it became evident that the University must either renounce the service of its most efficient members or be content to be served by laymen, he recognized that, at whatever sacrifice, a career must be provided into which a man could enter as his profession for life.

Another important question often present to his mind was the effect of the College system on the life and teaching of Oxford. He felt the difficulties as keenly as many who urged radical changes; but he felt likewise that it was worth making an effort to preserve this distinctive feature of the English Universities by transforming it to suit the new conditions. When in conversation he summed up the work of the Commission, it was, 'we have given a fresh lease of life to the College system.' He was not very sanguine that this system could be permanent, but he was convinced that it ought to have another chance, and that the best chance was secured to it by the reforms which he and his colleagues had effected.

It is difficult to speak of the charm of his life and conversation. The light touch and happy play of mind with which he enlivened the most serious business, and softened the jarring of controversy, was a source of real power, and procured a ready acceptance for the wisdom of his practical suggestions. In social life the same qualities shone forth at every moment. It seems hardly credible to those who knew him best that a deep-seated disease had been sapping his life for years. His temper was always unruffled, his spirits always gay and easy, and his sympathy always ready. In the midst of a mass of business which would have absorbed any ordinary man he could always find time to attend to the interests and concerns of his friends. To cheer a sick friend with the sunshine of his presence, to be the protector of the children of those who were taken away, to lend a ready ear to the perplexed and a helping hand to those who had committed themselves by any foolish action—all such kindnesses seemed so easy and natural to him, that men claimed and accepted his benefits almost as a matter of course. He seemed to be good not in obedience to any external law nor as the result of any internal struggle, but because goodness was the simple outcome of his nature.

His wit and gaiety were the delight of all who listened to him. It was not so much that he was a sayer of good things to be remembered and repeated—though of these too there was no lack—but the really characteristic feature of his talk was that its interest never flagged ; a certain flavour of freshness and originality pervaded it, and revealed itself even in his commonest remarks. To walk or ride with him was to enjoy a conversation in which not a sentence was commonplace. There was always some new light, some refinement or subtlety of thought or expression which gave a charm to the most ordinary topics. This effect was due mainly to the keen and delicate temper of his mind, but partly also to the wonderful breadth of his knowledge and his interests. He knew the literature of Greece and Rome as if he had made their study the work of his life, whereas it was really the amusement of his leisure hours. He had the sincerest love for the classical writings and the most profound belief in their value. His retentive memory and delicate taste made his conversation on these topics a storehouse of interesting and instructive criticism.

Though the resources of his own mind filled to overflowing every moment he could snatch for quiet study, yet he never shut himself up or held aloof from his fellows. There was absolutely nothing stern or forbidding about him. He seemed to take in the society of his friends the same pleasure which his presence imparted to them. In every relation of life there was in him the perfect ease

and grace which flows naturally from complete and sufficing strength. **The**
sweetness of his character and the perfect cordiality of his nature seemed
to offer all the rare gifts of his genius to minister to the happiness of his friends.
His death leaves dark what was a ray of sunlight in the lives of many.

He was entirely free from superstition. **He** held deliberately that the
questions whose solution is hidden from man, and above all the prospect of death,
should never be allowed to cast a shadow over the life and work of the present
hour. **He believed that** it became a man to live at his best and to labour at his
best during every day allotted to him, even as though an endless succession of
such days were in store. It was permitted to Henry Smith to give a bright
example of his theory. Till within a week of his death he was teaching from his
chair, attending to all the varied work of government and management for which
he was responsible, and living a bright and happy life which shed cheerfulness
and comfort on all around him. He always maintained, that there is no such
thing as a necessary man, and that every place left vacant can be adequately
filled. Of all that Henry Smith taught, this doctrine is the one which it seems
most difficult to realize **at this moment.**

[February, 1883.]

NOTE BY MR. ALFRED ROBINSON.

I HAVE been asked to give some account of the contested election in which
Professor Smith was a candidate for one of the University seats in the House of
Commons ; and I do this with much pleasure, because, although he was defeated,
the amount and kind of support which he received in the contest show how
much he was valued by men of all parties in Oxford, and how unique was his
position in the University.

In the spring of the year 1878 it became known that Mr. Gathorne Hardy,
who was then one of the University representatives, was about to be summoned
to the House of Lords. The rejection of Mr. Gladstone in 1865, and the defeat
of Sir Roundell Palmer by Sir John Mowbray in 1868, had proved that no one
but a Conservative could win in a contest conducted upon the lines of political
party. But it was thought by many persons that the Members for the University
ought to be chosen upon academical rather than upon political grounds, and
ought to represent learning, science, and education, without special reference to
party interests.

Professor Henry Smith was brought forward as a man most eminently qualified to represent the University in this sense. The fact that he was a Liberal in politics of course was not disguised. He was indeed at this time not fully in sympathy with some of the Liberal leaders. The Eastern question then filled the political foreground, and Professor Smith, while disapproving of the general policy of the Conservative Government, thought that Lord Salisbury ought to be supported in maintaining against Russia in her dealings with Turkey, the rights of the neutral Powers and the general interests of Europe. Perhaps, also, Professor Smith was too critical, and too fond of looking at questions from every point of view to have ever made a first-rate party man. But still he belonged undeniably to the Liberal party, and he was not a man to be led by any waywardness, or by any love of fads or crotchets, into a position of political isolation. So his election by the University would no doubt have been a transfer of a seat from the Government to the Opposition side of the House, and this was the aspect in which the contest presented itself to the great majority of the voters. It was not, however, on a contest of this kind that Professor Smith's chief supporters wished to enter. In their view the special representation of the University in Parliament was useless if the University Members were to be party men of the ordinary type, without special qualifications for dealing with the questions with which the University was specially concerned, and their main object in bringing forward Professor Smith was that this view should be put before the constituency and the country.

With the arrangements for his own candidature Professor Smith had very little to do. An old custom of the University, which had been observed by Mr. Gladstone throughout his long tenure of his seat, precluded a candidate from issuing any address, or from making any speech to the electors. At an early stage in the proceedings Professor Smith was invited to stand, and he agreed to allow himself to be nominated, but he took no part in the initiation of his own candidature ; he was never present at the meetings of his committee ; and his supporters defrayed the expenses of the contest, declining a request which he made that he might at least be permitted to contribute to the subscription list.

Professor Smith's Committee was formed in the month of April, 1878, and consisted of two sections.

(1) The London Committee, the Chairman of which was Mr. Mountague Bernard ; and which had for its Vice-Chairmen the then Marquis of Tavistock, Mr. Goschen, Mr. Knatchbull Hugessen (afterwards Lord Brabourne), Mr. Dodson

(now Lord Monk Bretton), Dean Stanley, the Dean of Canterbury, the Dean of Durham, and the late Sir Benjamin Brodie ; and for its Secretaries, Mr. Buller of All Souls, Mr. Ilbert, late Bursar and Fellow of Balliol, Mr. Pope, formerly Fellow of Lincoln, Mr. Robertson, Fellow of Corpus, Mr. A. L. Smith, then Fellow of Trinity.

(2) The Oxford Committee, having for its Chairman the Dean of Christ Church (Dr. Liddell) ; for its Vice-Chairmen, the then President of Corpus and Archdeacon Palmer ; and for its Secretaries, Mr. Crowder, Bursar of C. C. C., Professor Green, Mr. Jackson, Fellow and now Rector of Exeter, Mr. Monro, Fellow and now Provost of Oriel, Mr. Papillon, Fellow of New College, Mr. Salwey, Student of Christ Church.

It is not likely that any of these persons were under the illusion that their cause was going to win. The Conservative feeling of the constituency was soon found to be so strong that under no circumstances could any one but a Conservative have been elected. And at this time the excitement of the two political parties with reference to the Eastern Question much increased the difficulties with which Professor Smith's Committee had to contend. On the one hand, a large section of the constituency saw in him only an opponent of the Government which was patriotically defending British interests against Russia. And on the other, some well-known Liberals considered that he was too lukewarm in his censure of the Party and of the Ministry which they associated with the notorious atrocities in Bulgaria.

Opposition of the former kind, which insisted that the representative of the University of Oxford must be a supporter of a Conservative government, it was impossible to disarm. But an effort was made to conciliate the critics and opponents who belonged to the Liberal ranks. Professor Smith was requested by his Committee to put forward some definite statement of his views on the Eastern Question, and in the following letter to a member of his Oxford Committee he complied with this request.

DEAR ——,   *April 25, 1878.*

I am well aware that the custom of the University imposes a great measure of reserve upon any candidate for the honour of representing it in Parliament. But I do not think that I shall be departing from a tradition, which I am most anxious to see maintained, if I venture to write a few lines to you in explanation of the views which I entertain with regard to the Eastern Question.

There has been much in the foreign policy of the Government during the last two years of which I cannot approve. I think that they should have recognized, at a far earlier period than they did, that the condition of the Christian Provinces of Turkey bad become unendurable, and that the maintenance of the *status quo* was no longer possible. A grave, but long foreseen, emergency had arisen; and this country should have been prepared with a well-considered policy to meet it. Instead of this, the Ministry seem to me to have drifted with the stream of events, until at last they find themselves in a position in which it is immeasurably more difficult, than it would have been twelve months ago, to assert the right of the neutral powers to have a decisive voice in the settlement of a question affecting such vast European interests.

Looking at the most recent events, I have to express a general concurrence with the main tenor of Lord Salisbury's Despatch; and I have observed, with great satisfaction, that it has been received with cordial approval by the Liberal Press on the Continent. Interpreting that document, as I think I am justified in doing, by the light thrown on it by Lord Salisbury's own conduct at the Conference of Constantinople, I do not perceive in it any intention to restrict the liberties to be granted to the Christian subjects of the Porte; but I regard it as a protest in favour of the recognition of international obligations, and against any attempt on the part of Russia to dispose of the Eastern Question in her own way.

For the reasons which I have stated, I feel that I could not enter Parliament, except upon the condition of preserving the right to form while there an independent judgment with regard to the future action of the Government in these important matters. If there is a war party in England, I have no sympathy with it: but I am not for peace at any price; and, if any of the great interests of the country should be endangered, I should hope to see all Englishmen, without distinction of party, united in defending them.

Believe me to remain,

Very faithfully yours,

HENRY J. S. SMITH.

P.S.—You are at liberty to make any use which you may think fit of this reply to your letter.

This letter removed some of the misapprehensions as to Professor Smith's position, and probably produced some effect upon the canvass. Promises of support were received from some of the Liberals who had originally stood aloof, including one from Mr. Gladstone, which arrived a few days before the opening of the Poll. His example, however, was not imitated by all his followers, a few of whom, more Gladstonian than their chief, remained neutral to the last.

May 13th was fixed for the nomination. On that day the two candidates were proposed to the House of Convocation in Latin speeches—Professor Henry Smith by the Dean of Ch. Ch., Mr. J. G. Talbot by the President of St. John's. The Dean dwelt upon the scientific and literary qualifications of Professor Smith, his ability in business and in debate, and his suavity and fairness of judgment, which conciliated the regard of all. He recommended him to the electors as a man whom the Ministry of the day had entrusted with the most weighty

i

affairs, and as one 'unice idoneum qui ipse academicus academicos suos in Parlia-
mento repræsentet.' The President of St. John's, in nominating Mr. Talbot, made
some kindly remarks on the undesirableness of withdrawing Professor Smith
from the Professorial duties and from the sciences which he adorned.

Immediately after the nomination the Poll opened, and under the Act
governing University elections it was not to be closed until the 17th, unless
either of the candidates were withdrawn in the meantime.

The electors could vote either in person or by voting papers. At the time
when the voting began Professor Smith's Committee had received less than
a thousand promises from a constituency numbering more than four thousand
members, and the last hope of the most sanguine of his supporters had dis-
appeared. It was, however, thought best that all the votes should be recorded,
in order that the amount and kind of support with which his candidature had
been received might be accurately measured and generally known; so the
polling was continued daily for five days in all. At the close Mr. J. G. Talbot
was declared to be elected, the numbers being—Talbot, 2687; Smith, 989.

Defeated by a majority of more than two to one, Professor Smith's Committee
might to some extent console themselves with the thought that they had
conducted the contest with great economy. The expenses amounted to about
£420, the chief item being the bills for advertising the lists of supporters in the
chief London papers. This sum was less than half of what was believed to have
been spent on the Liberal side in each of the two preceding Oxford elections.

Still more consolatory was the analysis of the Poll Book, which was published soon after the result of the election was declared. This proved that the
majority of the electors and the working staff of the University had been ranged
under opposite banners. The following table shows how certain sections of the
constituency had voted :—

	SMITH.	TALBOT.	Abstained from voting.
Heads of Colleges, including two acting Heads......	10	10	3
Professors, Readers, and University Teachers.........	28	11	6
Tutors and Lecturers of Colleges and Halls	91	39	13
Fellows of Colleges, resident and non-resident	159	82	53
*Residents	152	117	44

* Residents—Members of Congregation qualified by residence—i. e. all electors who were in
residence Oct. 1876—Oct. 1877, including the parochial clergy in Oxford and others not engaged in
University work.

Whether this table points to any practical conclusion or not may be doubted. That the Members for the University should be chosen by those who are identified with it as the place of their work or residence in the present, and not merely of their education in the past, may seem reasonable, but no change could possibly be made which would reduce the constituency to less than one-tenth of its former number ; and perhaps the special representation of the Universities in Parliament is more likely in the future to be abolished than to be reformed.

But whatever inferences of this kind might be drawn from the result of the election, the Poll Book was unequivocal in its recognition of Professor Smith's personal qualifications and eminence. And even the numbers set forth in the foregoing table, emphatic as they are, do not fully express the estimation in which he was held by that portion of the constituency in the midst of which he had lived, and with which he had been officially connected. For among those who abstained from voting there were some who remained neutral, in spite of their high appreciation of his claims, because they thought that a seat in Parliament would be incompatible with his Oxford work ; and there were others who on ordinary occasions would have been ranked among his warmest supporters, but were unable at this time, when the foreign policy of the country filled the political horizon, to vote for a man who was variously criticised as going too far, or not far enough, in support of, or in opposition to, the Government of the day.

But, in spite of these abstentions, the preponderance of opinion in the working staff of the University was clearly marked, and was most significant.

It may be confidently said that no other man could have enlisted at this time among his supporters in a Parliamentary contest so many of the men who were identified by their position or occupation with Oxford ; and it may be doubted whether in any of the controversies, political and academic, which have divided the University at various times in its history, so many of its resident graduates have ever enrolled themselves upon one side.

i 2

INTRODUCTION

TO THE

COLLECTED MATHEMATICAL PAPERS

OF

HENRY J. S. SMITH.

THE present volumes contain all the mathematical papers published by the late Professor H. J. S. Smith in his lifetime, as well as those which were in the press or which had been written out for printing. The reader is therefore in possession of all that he had already published, or had wholly or partially prepared for publication at the time of his death.

The arrangement of the papers is strictly chronological, the order being that of the date of reading or publication. The only partial exception is the Report on the Theory of Numbers, which is printed as a whole, although several other papers which follow it were published in the six years during which it was in progress. It is possible therefore by merely glancing over the titles of the papers to trace the course of Professor Smith's mathematical studies and tastes. The first two papers, written in 1851 and 1852, show that his mind was then occupied by Geometry. Within three years he published his first paper on the Theory of Numbers, consisting of a characteristic proof of Fermat's theorem that every prime number of the form $4n + 1$ is the sum of two squares. From this time until 1867 the printed papers relate almost exclusively to the Theory of Numbers. Then follow a number of geometrical papers. In the last years of his life he was occupied principally with the subject of Elliptic Functions. It will be seen therefore that his work falls into three distinct groups: (i) Geometry, (ii) Theory of Numbers, (iii) Elliptic Functions. From the fact that the two earliest papers relate to Geometry we may infer that this was the subject which originally proved most attractive to him. The first of these papers was written in the year in which he obtained the Senior Mathematical Scholarship, and only a little more than a year after his election to a Fellowship at Balliol. It would seem that about 1853 he commenced the study of the Higher Arithmetic, a subject which engaged his almost undivided attention for many years, and which was never afterwards quite absent from his thoughts. The short notes which bear the dates of 1854 and 1857 show the tendency of his mind at this time · and in 1859 the first part of his Report on the Theory of Numbers was contributed to the British Association. The subsequent instalments appeared in the annual volumes of the Association for 1860, 1861, 1862, 1863, and 1865. These reports, which contain in a very condensed form the result of an immense amount of research, are models of clear exposition and systematic arrangement. Besides the accounts there given of the work of others, many of the paragraphs contain results of his own. These original contributions are not, however, noted as such, and they can only be detected by those who are already well acquainted with the details of the subjects to which they belong.

During the preparation of this Report he carried out elaborate researches of his own in several important branches of the Higher Arithmetic. The principal investigations undertaken at this time, which were completed for publication, relate to systems of indeterminate linear equations and congruences and to the orders and genera of ternary quadratic forms containing more than three indeterminates. These memoirs appeared in the *Philosophical Transactions* for 1861 and 1867. He also contributed several shorter papers to the Proceedings of the same Society, which indicate much more extended investigation in the same field : one especially (No. xviii, vol. i.) consists merely of a brief statement of results which were obtained by means of a very long and delicate analysis.

A considerable part of the last instalment of the Report is concerned with arithmetical formulæ derived from Elliptic Functions, and it seems likely that it was in this way that he was first attracted to this Theory ; for his first published paper on the subject (No. xvi, vol. i.) bears the date 1866. The remaining papers included in the first volume relate to Geometry, principally homographic figures.

In the second volume (1869–1883) there is more Elliptic Functions and less Theory of Numbers : but the sequence of the papers no longer affords an indication of the author's train of thought : for, in the later years of his life, he was frequently compelled, by various circumstances, to leave the subject upon which he was engaged, in order to prepare for publication theorems and demonstrations that formed part of the many unfinished investigations stored up in his note-books.

The first paper in the second volume was a prize memoir for which, conjointly with another memoir, the Steiner prize of the Berlin Academy was awarded. The subject was announced in 1866, and the memoirs were to be sent in, each designated by a motto, before March 1, 1868 *. Four were received, and the prize of six hundred thalers was divided between Professor Smith and Dr. Hermann Kortum, of Bonn, the two memoirs being regarded as of equal merit. The report on the memoirs received, which was laid before the Academy by Professor Kummer on July 2, 1868, contained the following remarks relating to that sent in by Professor Smith :

'Die vierte, in französischer Sprache abgefasste Preisschrift mit dem Motto . "Haud facilem esse viam voluit" führt den Titel : "Mémoire sur quelques problèmes cubiques et biquadratiques," und ist in drei Abschnitte eingetheilt. Der erste Abschnitt beschäftigt sich mit der Theorie des Imaginären in der Geometrie, der zweite enthält verschiedene Methoden, die gemeinsamen Punkte zweier durch ihre Elemente gegebener Kegelschnitte mittels des Lineals, des Cirkels und eines festen Kegelschnitts zu construiren, in dem dritten Abschnitte endlich löst der Verfasser ausser einigen andern sogenannten kubischen und biquadratischen geometrischen Aufgaben namentlich das speciell in der Preisfrage hervorgehobene, die Curven vierten Grades betreffende Problem. Die ganze Arbeit zeichnet sich durch übersichtliche und systematische Behandlung des Stoffes aus. Der Verfasser macht bei seinen Constructionen, wie es in der Preisfrage verlangt wird, nur von den einfachsten erforderlichen und ausreichenden Hilfsmitteln Gebrauch, aber bei den Constructions-Methoden selbst hat er mehr auf gedankliche als auf praktische Einfachheit, mehr auf die vollständige Darlegung aller Gesichtspunkte als auf die Ausführung aller einzelnen Operationen sein Bestreben gerichtet. Dadurch ist es ihm gelungen, im zweiten Abschnitte das an sich dürftige und trockene Material in gediegener und interessanter Weise zu verarbeiten und im dritten Abschnitte die specielle dort behandelte Frage mit allgemeineren zu verknüpfen. Fast überall lässt die Arbeit zum Vortheil für ihren wissenschaftlichen Werth deutlich erkennen, dass der Verfasser zu seinen umfassenderen Untersuchungen durch algebraische Betrachtungen gelangt ist, deren genauer Zusammenhang mit dem Gegenstande der Preisfrage schon in deren Formulirung enthalten ist †.'

The origin of the long memoir on the Theta and Omega Functions—the last paper but one in the second volume—was as follows. At the end of 1873, or the

* The announcement of the subject was made in the following terms : ' Für diejenigen geometrischen Probleme, deren algebraische Lösung von Gleichungen von höherem als dem zweiten Grade abhängt, fehlt es noch an der Feststellung der zur constructiven Lösung derselben erforderlichen und ausreichenden fundamentalen Hilfsmittel, so wie an den Methoden zur systematischen Benutzung dieser Hilfsmittel.

' Indem die Akademie die Frage, die sie stellt, auf die Probleme beschränkt, welche auf kubische Gleichungen führen, wünscht sie, dass wenigstens an einer Anzahl von speciellen Beispielen gezeigt werde, wie diese Lücke in dem Gebiete der constructiven Geometrie ausgefüllt werden könne. Namentlich verlangt sie die vollständige Lösung des folgenden Problems :

' Wenn dreizehn Punkte in der Ebene gegeben sind, so sollen durch geometrische Construction diejenigen drei Punkte bestimmt werden, welche mit den gegebenen zusammen ein System von sechzehn Durchschnittspunkten zweier Curven vierten Grades bilden.

' Bei der Lösung sind die Fälle zu berücksichtigen, in welchen einige der dreizehn Punkte imaginär und demgemäss nicht als individuelle Punkte, sondern als Durchschnittspunkte vorgelegter Curven gegeben sind. Gewünscht wird ferner, dass sämmtliche geometrische Constructionen durch die entsprechenden algebraischen Operationen erläutert werden.'

† *Monatsberichte* for 1868, p. 420.

beginning of 1874, when I was passing through the press the Tables of the
Theta Functions which I had calculated in connexion with a Committee of
the British Association, I asked Professor Smith, who was a member of the
Committee, if he would contribute an Introduction to the volume. He replied
that he did not see his way to writing anything appropriate to the tables
themselves, but that he 'could say something with respect to the constants
at the head of the pages.' These constants were K, K', E, J, J', &c., the
numerical values of which were given for every minute of the modular angle.
The memoir grew in extent, and was subject to frequent interruptions ;
in fact a number of other papers were written and published during its
progress. These papers were generally called into existence by special circumstances unconnected with the memoir, but a few of them, and especially
the Notes on the Transformation of Elliptic Functions (Nos. xli, xlii, vol. ii.),
which immediately precede it in the volume, arose directly out of it. The
first two of these Notes were given to me in the summer and autumn of 1882
for the *Messenger of Mathematics*, and appeared in the numbers from August
to November of that year. The remaining Notes were printed after his death
from a draft manuscript which he had shown to me, and explained in some
detail, in October, 1882. The memoir itself, with the Notes that were connected with it, formed the principal new work upon which he was engaged
from the time of its commencement until his death : most of the other papers,
published in the interval, containing results which were mainly derived from his
earlier investigations. It was left incomplete : Arts. 1–31 (pp. 415–484) had
been passed for press : Arts. 32–48 (pp. 485–535) had been revised, and Arts.
49–73 (pp. 535–585) were in type in quarto pages and had been partially
corrected. The succeeding Articles up to Art. 88 inclusive were in type in
octavo slip, and had been partially corrected in this form *. The last two
Articles (89 and 90) are printed from a manuscript found among his papers, and
which he had marked as following on after Art. 88. I believe that no more
was written, even in draft. The figures which occur in the Memoir had not
been drawn.

The object of Professor Smith's first paper on Elliptic Functions (No. xvi,

---

* The whole of the Memoir was originally set up all in octavo slip, and remained in this form for
a long time, during which it was greatly altered and extended. It was reset in quarto pages
during 1881 and 1882, and passed for press in this form. It had been intended that it should appear
as an Introduction, but it was finally decided that it should follow the tables with the title ' Memoir
on the Theta and Omega Functions.'

vol. i.) was, as stated in the first paragraph, to enunciate and demonstrate a fundamental theorem, the nature of which had been indicated in a letter, written in 1845, from Jacobi to M. Hermite, in which he mentioned that he used it as the starting-point in his Königsberg lectures. Jacobi died in 1851, and as the theorem referred to had never been published, Professor Smith reproduced it, in 1866, in this paper. Guided by Jacobi's suggestion, he multiplied together four general Theta series and expressed the product as the sum of four terms, each of which was the product of four Theta series with different arguments. From this theorem he derived, as indicated by Jacobi, all the principal results of Elliptic Functions, either as particular cases or as simple corollaries. In 1881 the first volume of the Collected Works of Jacobi was issued, and his Königsberg lectures on Elliptic Functions were there printed for the first time. By comparing them with Professor Smith's paper it will be seen that, although the theorem itself is of course essentially the same, still there are differences in the mode in which it is presented which enhance the interest of the latter. Professor Smith treated the question with great generality, and with absolute precision, and this short paper is very characteristic of his style of work.

At the meeting of the London Mathematical Society on January 8, 1879, Professor Cayley communicated to the Society the theorem

$$k^2 k'^2 \operatorname{sn} a \operatorname{sn} \beta \operatorname{sn} \gamma \operatorname{sn} \delta - k^2 \operatorname{cn} a \operatorname{cn} \beta \operatorname{cn} \gamma \operatorname{cn} \delta + \operatorname{dn} a \operatorname{dn} \beta \operatorname{dn} \gamma \operatorname{dn} \delta - k'^2 = 0,$$

where a, β, γ, δ are any quantities whose sum is zero. Professor Smith, who was present at the meeting, remarked that it was a special case of a theorem relating to the multiplication of four Theta functions, and at the next meeting in February he communicated to the Society the general Theta Function formulæ which dominate all results of this class. This paper (No. xxxviii, vol. ii.), which is supplementary to that of 1866, was written out from notes which he had had by him since that date.

The paper on the conditions of perpendicularity in a parallelepipedal system (No. xxxii, vol. ii.) was written in response to a request from his friend Professor Maskelyne, who was seeking for a general treatment of a problem which, in the particular case of its application to crystallography and the distribution of molecules in a crystal, was of paramount importance.

The circumstances connected with the publication of the memoir which concludes the second volume require a more extended notice. In February, 1882, he was surprised to see in the *Comptes Rendus* that the subject proposed by the French Academy for the Grand Prix des Sciences Mathématiques was the decomposition of a number into five squares *. His feelings in the matter are shown by the following extracts from letters to myself. In the first, dated Oxford, February 17, 1882, he wrote—'The Paris Academy have set for their Grand Prix for this year the theory of the decomposition of numbers into five squares, referring to a note of Eisenstein, *Crelle*, vol. xxxv, in which he gives without demonstration the formulæ for the case in which the number to be decomposed has no square divisor. In the Royal Society's Proceedings, vol. xvi, pp. 207, 208, I have given the complete theorems, not only for five, but also for seven squares : and though I have not given my demonstrations, I have (in the paper beginning at p. 197) described the general theory from which these theorems are corollaries with some fulness of detail. Ought I to do anything in the matter? My first impression is that I ought to write to Hermite, and call his attention to it. A line or two of advice would really oblige me, as I am somewhat troubled and a little annoyed ;' and in the second, of date February 22, he proceeded, ' You see I take your advice entirely upon the point that he ought to be written to. The worst of it is that it would take me a year, and a hundred pages, to work out the demonstrations of the paper in the Royal Society's Proceedings.'

The following reply was received from M. Hermite :

Mon cher Monsieur,

Aucun des membres de la commission qui a proposé pour sujet du prix des sciences mathématiques en 1882 la démonstration des théorèmes d'Eisenstein sur la décomposition des nombres en cinq carrés n'avait connaissance de vos travaux contenant depuis bien des années cette démonstration et dont j'ai pour la première fois connaissance par votre lettre. L'embarras n'est point pour vous, mais pour le rapporteur des mémoires envoyés au concours, et si j'étais ce rapporteur je n'hésiterais pas un moment à faire d'abord l'aveu complet de l'ignorance où il s'est trouvé de vos publications, et ensuite à proclamer hautement que vous aviez donné la solution de la question proposée. Une circonstance pourrait ôter tout embarras et rendre sa tâche facile autant qu'agréable. S'il avait en effet à rendre compte d'un mémoire adressé par vous-même dans lequel vous rappelleriez vos anciennes recherches en les complétant, vous voyez que justice vous serait rendue en même temps que les intentions de l'Académie

---

* The subject of the prize for **1882** had also been announced a year previously, but the notice had then escaped his attention. The following are the terms of the announcement :

Grand Prix des Sciences Mathématiques. (Prix du Budget.) Question proposée pour l'année 1882. L'Académie propose pour sujet du prix la *Théorie de la décomposition des nombres entiers en une somme de cinq carrés*, en appelant particulièrement l'attention des concurrents sur les résultats extrêmement remarquables énoncés sans démonstration par Eisenstein dans une Note écrite en langue française au Tome 35 du *Journal de Mathématiques de Crelle* (p. 368, année 1847).
' Le prix consistera en une médaille de la valeur de trois mille francs.
' Les Mémoires devront être remis au Secrétariat avant le 1er juin 1882 : ils porteront une épigraphe ou devise répétée dans un billet cacheté qui contiendra le nom et l'adresse de l'auteur. Ce pli ne sera ouvert que si la pièce à laquelle il appartient est couronnée.' (*Comptes Rendus*, vol. xcii. p. 622, March 14, 1881, and vol. xciv. p. 330, Feb. 6, 1882.)

seraient remplies puisqu'on lui annoncerait la solution complète de la question proposée. Jusqu'ici je n'ai pas eu connaissance qu'aucune pièce ait été envoyée, ce qui s'explique par la direction du courant mathématique qui ne se porte plus maintenant vers l'arithmétique. Vous êtes seul en Angleterre à marcher dans la voie ouverte par Eisenstein. M. Kronecker est seul en Allemagne : et chez nous M. Poincaré, qui a jeté en avant quelques idées heureuses sur ce qu'il appelle les invariants arithmétiques, semble maintenant ne plus songer qu'aux fonctions Fuchsiennes et aux équations différentielles. Vous jugerez s'il vous convient de répondre à l'appel de l'Académie à ceux qui aiment l'Arithmétique ; en tout cas soyez assuré que la commission aura par moi connaissance de vos travaux si elle a se prononcer et à faire un rapport à l'Académie sur des mémoires soumis à son examen ... Je vous renouvelle, mon cher Monsieur, l'expression de ma plus haute estime et de mes sentiments bien sincèrement dévoués.

CH. HERMITE.

Paris, 26 Février, 1882.

In consequence of an accident when riding, Professor Smith had been confined to his sofa for some weeks ; but, as far as his strength permitted, he had been working steadily at subjects connected with the memoir on the Theta and Omega subjects, which he was very reluctant to lay aside. Nevertheless, he thought it his duty to accede to the suggestion of M. Hermite, and bring his demonstrations before the Academy in the form of a memoir sent in for the *concours*. For a while he divided his spare time between Elliptic Functions and the work connected with the prize subject, but in April he wrote : 'I fear I cannot let you have the Transformation papers before the end of June. As I foresaw, getting the quadratic forms of n indeterminates into my mind again, putting my proofs into a rigorous form, and writing them out, will take up every moment till the end of May (the paper has to be in Paris by June 1). My sole reason for taking this trouble is that sooner or later I should have had to do it unless I was to allow my demonstrations to perish.'

Professor Smith died on February 9, 1883, and it was not till nearly two months after his death (at the meeting of the Academy on April 2) that the report of the Commission was announced, two prizes being awarded, one to Professor Smith and one to M. Minkowski, of Königsberg. The following is the text of the report :

Grand Prix des Sciences Mathématiques (Prix du Budget).

(Commissaires : MM. Hermite, Bonnet, Bertrand, Bouquet ; Jordan, rapporteur.)

L'Académie avait proposé pour sujet de prix la ' Théorie de la décomposition des nombres entiers en une somme de cinq carrés,' en appelant particulièrement l'attention des concurrents sur les résultats extrêmement remarquables énoncés sans démonstration par Eisenstein dans une Note écrite en langue française au tome 35 du *Journal de Mathématiques de Crelle*, p. 868, année 1847.

Ce problème semble assez restreint au premier **abord ; mais** on avait lieu de penser que les théorèmes obtenus par cet illustre géomètre s'étaient offerts à lui comme conséquences dernières d'une longue série de recherches, où devaient se trouver combinées les notions d'*ordre* et de *genre*, établies par Gauss pour les formes binaires, et transportées par Eisenstein dans le domaine des formes ternaires, celle de la *densité*, qu'il avait introduite pour la première fois, enfin les méthodes infinitésimales de Dirichlet. L'Académie était donc fondée à espérer que ce voyage de découvertes imposé aux concurrents à travers une des régions les plus intéressantes et les moins explorées de l'Arithmétique produirait des résultats féconds pour la Science. Cette attente n'a pas été trompée.

Trois Mémoires ont été transmis au Concours ; ils portent les épigraphes suivantes :

No. 1. Quotque quibusque modis possint in quinque resolvi
          Quadratos numeri, pagina nostra docet.

No. 2. **Felix** qui potuit rerum cognoscere causas !

No. 3. Rien n'est beau que le vrai ; le vrai seul **est aimable.**

Le **Mémoire** No. 2 montre chez son auteur des connaissances étendues **et** renferme plusieurs résultats intéressants ; mais la question posée par l'Académie ne s'y trouve même pas abordée. **La** Commission a donc principalement concentré son étude sur les deux autres Mémoires. **Tous deux sont** des œuvres considérables, où se trouvent exposés d'une manière magistrale plusieurs des points fondamentaux de la théorie des formes quadratiques. Les formules relatives à la décomposition en cinq carrés n'y figurent que comme conséquences très particulières des principes généraux.

Il est d'ailleurs aisé de discerner dans ces deux Mémoires, à travers les différences d'exposition, une singulière identité dans la filiation des idées, au point qu'il serait difficile de signaler dans l'un d'eux une notion ou un théorème important qu'on ne retrouvât pas dans l'autre, et que, pour éviter les redites et faire mieux ressortir les nuances qui les séparent, nous devions les analyser simultanément.

L'auteur du Mémoire No. 1 montre tout d'abord qu'à **une forme quadratique** quelconque on peut associer une série de formes adjointes * ; la valeur numérique **du plus grand** commun diviseur des coefficients de ces diverses formes et leur ordre de parité servent **de base à une** distribution en ordres de même déterminant.

L'auteur du Mémoire No. **3** ne parle pas **de ces formes** adjointes, si ce n'est de la première, que Gauss avait déjà définie ; **mais il considère la série** de leurs coefficients, ce qui **lui** donne un résultat **identique au précédent.** La marche suivie dans les deux Mémoires est d'ailleurs la même et consiste **à transformer la forme proposée en une autre** équivalente, telle que son résidu par rapport à un module **donné soit ramené à une expression canonique.**

Cette **expression canonique contient encore des coefficients** indéterminés dont la valeur dépendra **de la manière de conduire les calculs ;** mais de quelque façon que l'on opère, en partant d'une **forme donnée, certaines combinaisons** de ces coefficients conserveront toujours un caractère quadratique **déterminé par rapport aux** nombres premiers qui divisent le déterminant et par rapport aux nombres **4 et 8.** L'ensemble de ces caractères, invariables pour toutes les formes d'une même classe, définira le **genre.**

Ainsi que **Gauss** l'avait déjà signalé pour les formes binaires, **en** insistant tout particulièrement **sur ces** circonstances, qui sont pour l'Arithmétique du plus haut **intérêt, toutes les** combinaisons de caractères ne sont pas admissibles. Les **deux** auteurs indiquent d'une façon précise les conditions que doit remplir une semblable combinaison pour correspondre à un genre réellement existant.

Ils passent ensuite à la recherche **du nombre** des solutions des congruences du second degré à plusieurs inconnues. Cette question se lie intimement aux précédentes. La méthode élégante fondée sur l'emploi **de la** résolvante de Lagrange, **par** laquelle elle est traitée dans le Mémoire No. 3, mérite

---

* Ces formes avaient déjà été considérées **par M.** Darboux dans le *Journal de Liouville.*

une mention particulière. L'Auteur énonce ensuite cette proposition, dont il est facile de rétablir la démonstration : *Deux classes de formes qui appartiennent au même genre sont congrues par rapport à un module quelconque.*

Cette nouvelle définition du genre, déjà formulée d'ailleurs par M. Poincaré, a l'avantage de s'étendre immédiatement aux formes d'ordre supérieur au second.

Les deux auteurs s'occupent ensuite de la représentation des nombres par une forme quadratique à n variables. Ils montrent, en généralisant une méthode de Gauss, que cette recherche revient à celle de la représentation d'une forme quadratique à n—1 variables. Abordant ensuite ce dernier problème, ils font voir comment l'ordre et le genre de la forme représentée peuvent se déduire de l'ordre et du genre de la forme qui la représente. Les résultats précédents leur permettent de ramener la recherche de la densité des représentations d'un nombre donné par l'ensemble des formes d'un même genre à celle de la densité d'un genre donné.

L'application des méthodes de Dirichlet a fourni la solution de ce problème à l'auteur du Mémoire No. 1 pour les formes quaternaires ; à celui du Mémoire No. 3 pour les formes à un nombre quelconque de variables dont toutes les adjointes sont des formes impaires. Mais chacun d'eux, pressé par le temps, n'a donné la démonstration de ses résultats qu'autant qu'il était nécessaire pour résoudre le problème posé par l'Académie. Tous les deux les ramènent à la sommation d'une série infinie,

$$\sum \left(\frac{M}{m}\right)\frac{1}{m^s},$$

fort analogue à celle que Dirichlet avait rencontrée dans son célèbre Mémoire sur les applications du Calcul infinitésimal à la Théorie des nombres.

L'auteur de Mémoire No. 3 s'arrête à ce point ; celui du Mémoire No. 1 donne sans démonstration le résultat de la sommation, d'où découlent immédiatement les théorèmes d'Eisenstein.

De même que nous n'avons pu séparer ces deux beaux Mémoires dans la courte analyse qui précède, nous ne saurions les présenter l'un sans l'autre aux suffrages de l'Académie. Tous deux en sont également dignes. Ils font faire un pas considérable à l'Arithmétique, en fixant d'une manière définitive la théorie de l'ordre et du genre dans les formes quadratiques. Le talent déployé par les auteurs nous est d'ailleurs garant qu'ils sauront mener à terme les questions difficiles qu'ils ont dû traiter un peu hâtivement à la fin de leur travail.

Dans l'impossibilité où elle se trouve de mettre l'un d'eux au second rang, la Commission à l'unanimité émet le vœu que l'Académie accorde à chacun d'eux la totalité du prix, si elle le juge possible. Nous devons faire observer, en terminant, que le Mémoire No. 3 est écrit en allemand, contrairement à l'une des conditions du programme. L'auteur s'en excuse dans sa Préface, en disant que le temps lui a manqué pour faire la traduction de son Mémoire. Nous n'avons pas pensé qu'il y eût lieu de repousser *a priori*, pour une irrégularité de forme, un travail de cette importance. Mais, tout en l'accueillant, à titre exceptionnel, l'Académie devra faire toutes réserves pour l'application des règles ordinaires aux concours à venir.

L'Académie adopte les propositions de la Commission et décide qu'elle décernera deux prix de même valeur aux auteurs des Mémoires inscrits sous les Nos. 1 et 3.

Conformément au Règlement, M. le Président procède à l'ouverture des plis cachetés qui accompagnent ces Mémoires et proclame pour le No. 1 le nom de M. J. S. Smith, professeur à l'Université d'Oxford, et pour le No. 3 nom de M. Hermann Minkowski, étudiant de Mathématiques à l'Université de Königsberg.

It will be seen that in this report, which has been reproduced in its entirety, no mention is made of Professor Smith's previous publications, nor is there even a reference to his having completed Eisenstein's formulæ for five squares, and given the corresponding formulæ for seven squares, more than fifteen years before : in fact, the report shows that the writer regarded Professor Smith's memoir as perfectly new work called into existence by the prize competition. Under these circumstances Miss Smith, as the representative of her brother, wrote to M. Hermite recalling his attention to the expression in his letter of February 26, 1882, ' En tout cas soyez assuré que la commission aura par moi connaissance de vos travaux si elle a se prononcer et à faire un rapport à l'Académie sur des mémoires soumis à son examen,' and expressing the hope that he would give the explanation that had become necessary.   M. Hermite replied that the omission of which she complained was an error which was due to absolutely involuntary forgetfulness (' ce tort ne consiste que dans un oubli, qui a été absolument invo- lontaire') ; but he made no further statement of any kind.   The award of the prize gave rise however to a good deal of comment in the Paris newspapers.   The Academy was blamed for having been unaware of work published by the Royal Society in 1868, and it was pointed out that the award was necessarily unsatis- factory, in spite of Professor Smith himself having sent in a memoir, as any other competitor might have availed himself of the indications contained in his published writings.   The striking identity between the first and third memoirs, which is emphasized in the report, gave rise to the statement, which appeared in the newspapers, that this had actually taken place.   In consequence of these criticisms M. Bertrand made certain explanations at the meeting of the Academy on April 16, 1883.   The proceedings commenced with the reading of an appreciative obituary notice of Professor Smith by M. Camille Jordan, in which special reference was made to his arithmetical researches.   The account then proceeds :

M. Bertrand demande à l'Académie la permission d'ajouter quelques mots à la lecture qu'elle vient d'entendre.

' La Commission chargée de proposer le sujet du prix de Mathématiques avait demandé aux concurrents l'étude d'un théorème énoncé, il y a près de quarante ans, par l'illustre géomètre Eisenstein, enlevé à la science avant d'en avoir publié la démonstration.

' Un seul Mémoire depuis la mort d'Eisenstein avait été consacré à cette difficile question : il était de M. Smith et, comme celui d'Eisenstein, contenait l'énoncé seulement des résultats principaux. Si le concours proposé par l'Académie n'était pas venu reporter l'attention de M. Smith vers ces recherches déjà anciennes, il n'aurait, de même qu'Eisenstein, légué sur ce sujet aux géomètres qu'un énigme difficile à déchiffrer.

' Sur les trois Mémoires présentés au concours, le premier a été écarté comme insuffisant.

' Le deuxième suivait exactement la marche tracée par M. Smith et donnait la démonstration de ses énoncés ; celui des Commissaires qui a accepté la tâche d'en faire l'examen a pu, sur ces indices, deviner le nom de l'auteur. Peu importait, d'ailleurs, que le Mémoire fût de M. Smith ou inspiré par le travail depuis longtemps livré au public par le savant professeur d'Oxford : **il méritait incontestablement le prix.**

' Un troisième Mémoire résolvait la question ; il était **difficile que** deux géomètres assez **habiles** pour parcourir ce terrain élevé, mais un peu étroit, ne s'y rencontrâssent pas sur plus d'un point. **Les** méthodes avaient de l'analogie, mais chaque Mémoire portait la marque d'un esprit original et distingué ; tous deux étaient excellents et il semblait impossible de **donner** à l'un d'eux le second **rang.**

' **Les** deux Mémoires seront publiés, et l'Académie se félicitera d'avoir donné **à leurs savants auteurs, l'un à la fin,** l'autre au début **de** sa carrière, l'occasion **de montrer les ressources d'un esprit ingénieux et la** preuve, inscrite à chaque page, d'une science étendue et profonde.'

These official remarks, which are supplementary to the report of the Commission, render justice to M. Minkowski, and offer a carefully framed defence of the Academy, but without admitting that the subject was proposed in ignorance of Professor Smith's work, or that the reporter was not aware of the existence of the paper of 1867 until after the publication of the report. In a historical statement relating to the subject and award of the prize, drawn up a fortnight after the publication of the report, and in reply to adverse criticisms, a full avowal of all the circumstances might have been looked for. It is right to say that M. Camille Jordan, the reporter, was not a member of the Academy when the subject was announced, and that it was only at the last moment that he was charged with the duty of reporting upon the three memoirs.

It is much to be regretted that it should have been necessary to devote so much space to the matters connected with this memoir. A very brief notice would have sufficed if M. Hermite had communicated the existence of the paper of 1867 to the other members of the Commission, or if after the award he had given a brief account of the facts, or caused such an account to be given. But the only statement made was that of M. Bertrand, and it therefore became impossible to avoid details and quotations, as Professor Smith would not have been willing to send in a memoir for the competition except under the special circumstances of the case and in response to M. Hermite's suggestion.

An Appendix at the end of the second volume contains four writings which, though not of the same original character as the papers themselves, necessarily find a place in a collected edition of Professor Smith's mathematical works. The last of the four is a portion of the Introduction to the collected edition of Clifford's Mathematical Papers, which was written in the summer of 1881. Only so much of this Introduction has been included as could be of interest to a reader who had not the book itself before him. A reference should be here added to a review by Professor Smith of Campbell and Garnett's *Life of Professor*

Clerk Maxwell which appeared in the *Academy* for January, 1883 (vol. xxiii, pp. 19, 35). This review, being almost wholly biographical, is not reprinted.

He contributed verbally to the meetings of the London Mathematical Society and British Association a number of papers, which unfortunately were never written out. The following is a list of the titles of these papers :

London Mathematical Society.

1. Construction of the last point of intersection of a cubic curve by a curve of a superior order. March 26, 1868 (vol. ii, p. 61).
2. Geometrical note on the concomitants of a binary cubic. March 26, 1868 (vol. ii, p. 61).
3. Theory of certain systems of conics which present themselves in connexion with cubic curves. May 28, 1868 (vol. ii, p. 67).
4. On a problem in kinematics, and focal properties of skew surfaces. April 14, 1870 (vol. iii, p. 99).
5. On elliptic integrals. December 8, 1870 (vol. iii, p. 195).
6. On skew cubics. March 9, 1871 (vol. iii, p. 224).
7. On the partition of geometrical curves. February 10, 1876 (vol. vii, p. 90).
8. On the aspects of circles on a plane or on a sphere. April 13, 1876 (vol. vii, p. 179).
9. On some elliptic function properties. January 11, 1877 (vol. viii, p. 139).
10. On Eisenstein's Theorem. June 14, 1877 (vol. viii, p. 289).
11. Note relating to the theory of the division of the circle. April 11, 1878 (vol. ix, p. 102).
12. On a correction in Sohncke's tables. January 9, 1879 (vol. x, p. 44).
13. Upon a modular equation. January 9, and February 13, 1879 (vol. x, pp. 42 and 75).
14. Two geometrical notes relating to surfaces of the second order. March 13, 1879 (vol. x, p. 104).
15. Two geometrical notes. June 12, 1879 (vol. x, p. 167).
16. Geometrical notes (3). February 12, 1880 (vol. xi, p. 50).

British Association.

1. On a property of surfaces of the second order	1866, p. 6.	Nottingham.
2. On the large prime numbers calculated by Mr. Barrett Davis	1866, p. 6.	,,
3. On a construction for the ninth cubic point	1868, p. 10.	Norwich.
4. On geometrical constructions involving imaginary data	1868, p. 10.	,,
5. On a property of the Hessian of a cubic surface	1868, p. 10.	,,
6. On the circular transformation of Möbius	1872, p. 24.	Brighton.
7. On modular equations	1873, p. 24.	Bradford.
8. On singular solutions	1875, p. 21.	Bristol.
9. On the effect of quadric transformation on the singular points of a curve	1875, p. 21.	,,
10. On the modular curves	1878, p. 463.	Dublin.
11. On quadric transformation	1878, p. 465.	,,
12. On inverse figures in geometry	1880, p. 476.	Swansea.
13. On a mathematical solution of a logical problem	1880, p. 476.	,,
14. On the distribution of circles on a sphere	1880, p. 476.	,,

I have omitted a title from this list whenever I knew that the paper in question was published elsewhere. Thus a paper 'On Continued Fractions' which was communicated to the British Association in 1875 was afterwards published in the *Messenger*, and forms No. xxviii. of the present reprint. It is probable that the contents of a few others are included in the published papers. No doubt all the results upon which these communications were founded are contained in his note-books.

With respect to the character of Professor Smith's mathematical writings a very noticeable feature is the arithmetical spirit that runs through the whole of his work. The years of study which produced the Report upon the Theory of Numbers exercised a lasting influence upon his mode of thought; and his familiarity with the ideas and methods of the Higher Arithmetic continually shows itself in his treatment of Geometry and Elliptic Functions. In the latter subject the arithmetical tendency of his mind is especially evident in the point of view from which the theory of Transformation is always regarded. Another characteristic feature of his work is its completeness, both as regards attention to details and accuracy of demonstration. He had a very strong dislike to careless or slovenly work of any kind, and thought that it was nowhere so much out of place as in Pure Mathematics. He was ready enough to pass over the ground boldly and rapidly, without regard to ambiguities or details, when he was seeking after new theorems, or merely endeavouring to decide upon the truth of generalizations or guesses; but he was of opinion that a mathematician should refrain from publication until he had established his results by perfectly rigorous demonstration. He had no sympathy with those who were contented to give imperfect demonstrations, or to regard results as proved merely because they had satisfied themselves of their truth. No task is more irksome to a mathematician than that of working out in detail all the various particular cases of a theorem, when the novelty of the investigation by which it was discovered has long since worn off. The general result, too, of such examinations is to produce modifications and limitations which at the same time add to the cumbrousness of the demonstrations and detract from the simplicity of the theorems themselves. But he held that any slurring-over of difficulties or ambiguities was utterly repugnant to the nature of the subject, and that a mathematician was bound to spare no amount of labour that was requisite in order to give to his results the highest degree of precision of which they were susceptible. The comparatively slow rate of progress of the memoir on the Theta and Omega Functions was no doubt primarily due to the many other claims upon his time, but it was also attributable, in no slight degree, to the extreme care taken to avoid ambiguities of every kind, and to the attention bestowed upon the systematic examination of all the special cases of the general theorems. His natural love of precision in thought and expression was no doubt strengthened by his early study of the writings of Gauss, for whom he always felt the most unbounded admiration. The following notes, which he wrote for Mr. Tucker*, on the occasion of the celebration of the centenary of Gauss's birth, find a fitting place here, as they show, in his own words, not only his deep reverence for the great master of the Higher Arithmetic, but also the extreme importance that he attached to perfection of form in the presentation of mathematical results.

If we except the great name of Newton (and the exception is one which Gauss himself would have been delighted to make) it is probable that no mathematician of any age or country has ever surpassed Gauss in the combination of an abundant fertility of invention with an absolute rigorousness in demonstration, which the ancient Greeks themselves might have envied. It may be admitted, without any disparagement to the eminence of such great mathematicians as Euler and Cauchy, that they were so overwhelmed with the exuberant wealth of their own creations, and so fascinated by the interest attaching to the results at which they arrived, that they did not greatly care to expend their time in arranging their ideas in a strictly logical order, or even in establishing by irrefragable proof propositions which they instinctively felt, and could almost see, to be true. With Gauss the case was otherwise. It may seem paradoxical, but it is probably nevertheless true, that it is precisely the effort after a logical perfection of form which has rendered the writings of Gauss open to the charge of obscurity and unnecessary difficulty. The fact is that there is neither obscurity nor difficulty in his writings, as long as we read them in the submissive spirit in which an intelligent schoolboy is made to read his Euclid. Every assertion that is made is fully proved, and the assertions succeed one another in a perfectly just analogical order; there is nothing so far of which we can complain. But when we have finished the perusal, we soon begin to feel that our work is but begun, that we are still standing on the threshold of the temple, and that there is a secret which lies behind the veil and is as yet concealed from us. No vestige appears of the process by which the result itself was obtained, perhaps not even a trace of the considerations which suggested the successive steps of the demonstration. Gauss says more than once that, for brevity, he only gives the synthesis, and suppresses the analysis of his propositions. 'Pauca sed matura' were the words with which he delighted to describe the character which he endeavoured to impress upon his mathematical writings. If, on the other hand, we turn to a memoir of Euler's there is a sort of free and luxuriant gracefulness about the whole performance, which tells of

* 'Carl Friedrich Gauss,' by R. Tucker. *Nature*, vol. xv, p. 537 (April 19, 1877).

the quiet pleasure which Euler must have taken in each step of his work; but we are conscious nevertheless that we are at an immense distance from the severe grandeur of design which is characteristic of all Gauss's greater efforts. The preceding criticism, if just, ought not to appear wholly trivial; for though it is quite true that in any mathematical work the substance is immeasurably more important than the form, yet it cannot be doubted that many mathematical memoirs of our own time suffer greatly (if we may dare to say so) from a certain slovenliness in the mode of presentation; and that (whatever may be the value of their contents) they are stamped with a character of **slightness and perishableness**, which contrasts strongly with the **adamantine** solidity and clear hard modelling, which (we may be sure) will keep the writings of **Gauss from being forgotten** long after the chief results and methods contained in them have been incorporated in treatises more easily read, and have come to form a **part of the common** patrimony of all working mathematicians. And we must never forget (what in an **age so fertile of** new mathematical conceptions as our own, we are only too apt to forget) that it is the **business of mathematical** science not **only** to discover new truths and new methods, but also to establish **them, at whatever cost of time and** labour, upon a basis of irrefragable reasoning.

The μαθηματικὸς πιθανολογῶν has no more right to be listened to now than he had in the days of Aristotle; but it **must be owned** that since the invention of the 'royal roads' of analysis, defective modes of reasoning and of proof have had a chance of obtaining currency which they never had before. It is not the greatest, but it is perhaps not the least, of Gauss's claims **to the admiration of** mathematicians, that, while fully penetrated with a sense of the vastness of **the science, he exacted** the utmost rigorous**ness** in every part **of it, never** passed over a **difficulty as if it did not exist, and never** accepted a theorem as true beyond the limits within which it **could actually be demonstrated.**

These words certainly express the ideal which Professor Smith had always in his mind, and which has governed the character of his own work.

In passing the papers through the press I have corrected all the misprints and errors that I detected, but no other alterations of any kind have been made in the text. I have added notes only in those cases where they seemed to be absolutely necessary. All additions, references, or notes which are not in the original papers are enclosed in square brackets [ ]. The correction of misprints or slips often involved matters of some delicacy, and occasioned frequent delays. There were also other difficulties connected with the papers that were printed from manuscript. The sheets containing the concluding portion of the Report on the Theory of Numbers were passed through the press (during my absence abroad) by Professor Cayley, by whom the index to the Report was made. Professor Cayley also kindly undertook the revision of the uncorrected portion of the Memoir on the Theta and Omega Functions.

Professor Smith did not leave many separate mathematical manuscripts. most of his work being contained in note-books. These books, about forty in number, cover the whole period of his mathematical career. Some contain his early notes when making his first studies in Geometry, or reading the memoirs upon which the Report on the Theory of Numbers was founded; others relate to his University lectures; and rather more than a dozen are devoted to the

records of original work, a very large portion of which has never been published. I have repeatedly examined the note-books relating to the subjects
with which I was most familiar in hopes of being able to make extracts that
could have been included in the present volumes. But in this I have been
unsuccessful, for Professor Smith entered in these books not only the finished
theorems which he had demonstrated, but also results which he had arrived at by
rough explorations and inductions, as well as mere guesses sometimes ; and it is
certain that he would have published nothing himself from these books without
submitting it to the most careful examination and working out the demonstrations afresh. Under these circumstances it was decided, but with great
reluctance, to confine the present work to the published writings, and make no
attempt to give an account of the varied contents of the note-books. The editing
of any considerable portion of the unpublished work would be a matter of great
difficulty, requiring much time and research, but it would not be so serious an
undertaking to prepare separately for publication some of the investigations
which he has left upon special subjects. In particular, it is very desirable
that his researches relating to the decomposition of numbers into seven squares
should be published ; and it would probably be found that the editing of this
application of the general formulæ has been greatly simplified by his own treatment (in the prize memoir) of the corresponding work on the five-square problem.

The principal subjects upon which he lectured in the University were
Modern Geometry, Analytical Geometry, Theory of Numbers, Calculus of Varia-
tions, and Differential Equations. With the exception of the Theory of Numbers,
his lecture-notes on these subjects are very fragmentary; but full and accurate
transcripts of the lectures themselves as delivered were kindly supplied by
Mr. Lazarus Fletcher, F.R.S., Mr. Thiselton Dyer, F.R.S., Mr. H. T. Gerrans, Mr.
Walter Larden, the late Mr. Arthur Buchheim, and other pupils. As no other
teaching on Modern Geometry was given in an English University, and as his
lectures on this subject exercised great influence upon the direction of mathematical studies in Oxford, it was considered very important that they should be
published. The editorship was undertaken by Mr. H. M. Taylor, Fellow of
Trinity College, Cambridge, who after a careful comparison of the lectures as
delivered in different years wrote out for press a fair copy of what might be
regarded as the standard form of the course. It was, however, finally decided to
abandon the publication, partly because the same ground was more systematically
covered by foreign treatises, and partly because the extent of the lectures was
so limited (owing to the fact that students did not specialize in the subject) that

the volume would be scarcely adequate to form an independent treatise on so important a branch of Mathematics. It may be mentioned that the courses delivered in various years differed very much from one another, and it would appear as if their nature and extent had to some degree depended upon the audience.

It is well known that Professor Smith intended to write an Introduction to the Theory of Numbers, and regret was frequently expressed to him that the work was still unpublished. Among his note-books there are several in which the elements of the subjects are very clearly and succinctly explained in methodically arranged paragraphs, and it cannot be doubted that these are successive editions of the commencement of such a work, in which he was striving after greater perfection. Other note-books contain carefully written articles which may have been intended as chapters in such a work. The completed portion of the treatise, however, is so small, only reaching to quadratic forms, that the idea at first entertained of publishing it separately as a fragment was ultimately given up.

I hope that it will not be thought out of place for me to include in this Introduction a few reminiscences of my own with respect to Professor Smith, as he appeared to me, and to attempt a sketch, however slight, of his personality. In the eleven years that have elapsed since his death many of those to whom his presence was so familiar have passed away, and a new generation of mathematicians has arisen to whom he is but a name, so that the time seems to have already come when it is allowable to place on record matters which were once of common knowledge or might have seemed too trivial for mention in print.

I first saw Professor Smith at the British Association meeting at Nottingham in 1866, when he was one of the secretaries of Section A (Mathematics and Physics). I can perfectly remember his attitude and manner both when as secretary he read the papers of others, and when standing by the blackboard, he explained, so simply and gracefully, the nature of his own communications to the section. His tall handsome figure, his commanding presence, and the charm of his manners, stand out clearly before me, as I watched him then; and in no essential respect was there any change in him between the first time I saw him and the last.

At this meeting he spoke upon the average frequency of prime numbers, and I then for the first time heard of Legendre's approximate formula $\dfrac{x}{\log x - 1 \cdot 08366}$ for the number of primes inferior to x, a result which interested me intensely, although I little thought that it was subsequently to occupy so much of my own time *.

I was introduced to him in the committee-room of the section by my father, and although I was not eighteen years of age, he welcomed me with as much cordiality as if I had been a fellow-mathematician of equal standing with himself. I was a shy and retiring schoolboy, but, in spite of the respect with which his knowledge inspired me, his kind and friendly manner at once placed me at my ease. I mention so particularly this experience of my own because it was very characteristic of his gentle and considerate nature. I am sure that no one was ever treated by him with less courtesy or attention on account of youth or junior standing; on the contrary, I believe that in such cases he instinctively and unconsciously showed even more consideration. I may perhaps mention that on this occasion he gave me the first separate reprint of a mathematical paper which I ever possessed : it was not a paper of his own, but one which had been given to him, and seeing me interested in it he told me I might have it, as he could procure another copy from the author.

I did not see him again till the meeting of the British Association at Brighton in 1872, the year after that in which I took my degree at Cambridge. At that meeting he spoke upon the circular transformation of Möbius. I was then able for the first time to appreciate his wonderful power as an expositor of abstruse mathematics. His winning manners and graceful delivery charmed me as before, but I was even more struck with the skill with which he succeeded in giving, in the simplest language, a correct idea of complicated theories to those to whom they were entirely new.

---

* My memory is quite distinct that this account was given as a 'Report on the Theory of Numbers,' and that he briefly explained to the section the nature of the subjects dealt with in the report. This impression is confirmed by the fact that among the sectional papers there is no title under which Legendre's formula could have been introduced ; for the paper ' On the large prime numbers calculated by Mr. Barrett Davis ' (which I also distinctly remember), was given on a different day and in a different room. (Mr. Barrett Davis had communicated a manuscript list of large prime numbers, and Professor Smith, in laying them before the section, merely called attention to the fact that, as in the case of the smaller primes, they were sometimes clustered thickly together and sometimes widely separated.) It would therefore appear, almost with certainty, that Professor Smith had intended to write a seventh part of the report, which should relate to the frequency of primes and other asymptotic formulæ in the Theory of Numbers. The early note-books written while the report was in preparation contain references to Legendre's law, and a résumé of Lejeune Dirichlet's memoir on asymptotic formulæ in the Berlin Abhandlungen for 1849. Professor Plücker was present at this meeting, and exhibited some models of complexes to the section on the same morning as that on which Professor Smith spoke upon the subject of his Report.

All the papers of which he gave any verbal account in public after this date were communicated either to the London Mathematical Society or to Section A of the British Association, and I believe I was present on every such occasion; for I was a very regular attendant at the meetings of the Mathematical Society; and was one of the secretaries of Section A from 1871 to 1880 inclusive. I was also present at the meetings in 1881 and 1882. Several of these papers, like the one I have just referred to, related to subjects with which I was quite unfamiliar; but I never failed to derive some benefit from his explanations or to feel a deeper interest in the theories of Pure Mathematics in consequence of what he had said. In general I do not readily gain an insight into new mathematical methods merely from verbal explanations, but his papers had a wholly exceptional effect upon me in this respect. He had the gift of fixing the complete attention of his audience, and imparting valuable knowledge, no matter how remote or technical the subject. Those who were present at the reading of any paper of his will know that there is no exaggeration in this. Some mathematicians of our day have regarded the reading of a technical paper before a society as a mere formal preliminary to printing, which exists only as a survival from the past : but the beautiful mathematical expositions by which Professor Smith could gently lead on his audience into the remote intricacies of a difficult subject, prove that it is possible even in Pure Mathematics to convey a true idea of highly technical researches without being technical at all. He always began at a point from which an ordinary mathematical listener could take up the thread, and, laying down the main lines of his subject in a series of simple and clear sentences, following each other in logical order, succeeded, apparently with the greatest ease, in placing his audience in possession of sufficient general knowledge to enable them to grasp the nature and scope of the new work that he was bringing before them. He spoke slowly, with a marked emphasis and a measured and almost rhythmical utterance, which were very distinctive and attractive. His language was always peculiarly felicitous, both in formal expositions and in private conversation ; and the elegance of his style may be fairly judged by the papers printed in the Appendix, which, I think, those who knew him could scarcely read without fancying that they heard in them the cadence of his voice. Although dignified in words, manner, and bearing, he was utterly free from any trace of formality : and indeed no small part of the charm of his character was due to the way in which natural dignity was modified by sweetness of disposition and gaiety of heart. Even when explaining

the most abstract theories with the severest logical accuracy, his liveliness
and wit would frequently peep out unexpectedly in parenthetical remarks.
He was always in touch with his surroundings, but never more perfectly so
than when addressing a mathematical audience, for his modesty and unselfishness
rendered it impossible for him ever to weary others by allowing himself to
be carried away by the interest which he felt himself in the researches he
was explaining. On no single occasion was he ever dull or tedious, and his
papers were always looked forward to with pleasure at the Mathematical Society
and by the habitués of the mathematical Saturdays at the British Association
meetings. The power to render advanced researches intelligible and interesting
to a mixed audience is a rare gift; and the only other brilliant **expositor** of
mathematics whom I have ever heard was Clifford, whose style however differed
widely in almost every respect from that of Professor Smith. Clifford spoke very
rapidly and fluently, in cleverly-worded sentences that were often startling
or paradoxical. The art with which he could invest familiar things with
a new interest, or connect them with novel ideas, and the facility with which
this was done, apparently on the spur of the moment, were truly surprising, but
it seemed to me that the effect produced was greatly dependent upon the exact
words which he used and upon his mode of delivery. In Professor Smith's expositions there was never anything paradoxical or artificial. The explanations
which he gave were perfectly matter-of-fact, his power being shown in the skill
with which he held the sustained attention of his hearers as he proceeded from
step to step.

  It should be mentioned that very few of his papers were produced quite
spontaneously. Mr. Tucker, the secretary of the Mathematical Society, was always
anxious to have several communications announced for each meeting, and if he had
not received enough titles would write to those who were likely to have papers in
progress or suitable matter for verbal communication to the Society. Professor
Smith always responded willingly to such appeals, and would mention subjects upon
which 'he could say something, if required.' In the same way, at the meetings of the British Association at which he was present, I always asked him for
papers, and he would give me a list of subjects which he could bring before the
section, sometimes offering me a choice and letting me select those which I pre-
ferred. In making his verbal communications he generally placed one of his quarto
note-books on the table, open at the place, and occasionally referred to it as he
proceeded with his explanation. These quarto note-books in their greyish covers
were well-known objects to all who attended mathematical meetings between

1873 and 1883. After laying before the Mathematical Society the results of some researches of his own, probably carried out years before, great pressure would be brought to bear to induce him to write out an account which would be suitable for publication. This he did whenever he could find the time, but unfortunately many of his most interesting communications remained unwritten when death removed him. The communications to Section A were never intended to be published in the volumes of the Association. One he wrote out for me for the *Messenger* (No. xxviii, vol. ii.), and others which I had specially asked for had been promised to me for the same journal.

The address which he delivered before the Mathematical Society on retiring from his two years of office as President in 1876 possesses so much mathematical interest that I felt justified in including it among the papers (No. xxxi, vol. ii.). I think it would be admitted without question that this was by far the most remarkable presidential address, both in substance and in mode of delivery, which has been made to the Society.

I have been thus particular in trying to describe the characteristic features of his method of exposition, partly because for some years before his death there was no more conspicuous personal figure in English Mathematics, and partly because in the severe style of the papers themselves there is no trace of the bright and winning gaiety of manner with which their first introduction to a mathematical audience was so often adorned.

I should despair of the possibility of myself conveying any adequate impression of Professor Smith's position in University and general society, but fortunately I am saved from the anxiety of any such attempt by the excellent article in the *Spectator* from the accomplished pen of the late Lord Bowen, which is reprinted on pp. 50–55. This tribute of affectionate appreciation, in which Professor Smith's character is delineated with perfect justice and delicacy, enables the reader to form a true idea of the unique place which he held in the larger world in which he moved, while his special claims as a mathematician were unknown to all except a few experts. His general attainments were so great and varied, and his personal and social qualities so brilliant, that his mathematical powers were completely overshadowed by other more conspicuous gifts. In an article in the *Times*, published the day after his death, it was truly said : ' It is probable that of the thousands of Englishmen who knew Henry Smith, scarcely one in a hundred ever thought of him as a mathematician at all. . . . He was a classical scholar of wide knowledge and exquisite taste, and there were few who talked to him on English, French, German, or Italian literature, who were not struck by his extensive knowledge, his capacious memory, and his sound and critical judgment.'

It always seemed to me very strange that it should have been possible for him to have held so distinguished a position in the foremost rank of mathematicians without his eminence, or his devotion to the subject, becoming more widely recognized among his friends and colleagues. His official post in the University was that of Professor of Geometry, and it was of course well known that he was an accomplished mathematician of high reputation. But I am sure that very few even of his intimate friends were aware that in his own subjects he stood alone in England, and that his papers upon the Higher Arithmetic held a place among the most important productions of the century in abstract science. Even fewer still had any idea of the extent to which his heart and mind were engrossed by his mathematical researches. This want of recognition (if it may be so called) was no doubt partly due to his disinclination to speak of his own work except occasionally to those whom he knew to be interested in it, and his non-mathematical friends may be pardoned for not discovering an enthusiasm which showed itself so little ; in fact it cannot be doubted that he would have been spared much of the voluntary work which he so unselfishly undertook at the solicitation of others, if the depth of his devotion to his own subject had been generally known. But I think a truer explanation is to be found in the fact that, as his whole time and powers were apparently given up to other occupations, such as University work of all kinds and Royal Commissions, it could scarcely be supposed that he would be much more than a distinguished amateur in so exacting a science. There was nothing that suggested the specialist in his actions or conversation ; and it is indeed truly remarkable that, in the midst of so many varied pursuits all requiring constant care and attention, he should have been able to carry out original work which can compare in extent and profundity with the researches of the ablest mathematicians, who have concentrated their whole lives upon their special subjects. Except in vacations he seemed to have no time for mathematical investigation, and the amount that he accomplished was always a mystery to me until I learned that after a hard day's work, closing perhaps with a dinner party at which his lively wit and brilliant conversation had made him seem the gayest and the brightest of the circle, he would quietly settle down to work in his own room for some hours before going to bed. What he then wrote related probably to matters that had been more or less in his mind all day, and to which at intervals he had actively turned his thoughts, making a few stray notes perhaps on slips of paper. The last thing of all at night he would enter the results of the day's work or thoughts in his note book. Most of his mathematical work he did in his head, by sheer mental effort, and he scarcely ever committed an investigation to paper in any detail except when writing it out for publication. The notes which he made while thinking out a subject were often written on scraps of paper or backs of envelopes, which were destroyed as soon as he had made a definite advance which would allow of an entry in his notes. The fact that he used pen and paper so little, relying on his brain as it were, increased the mental strain of his mathematical production, so that, as a rule, when struggling with difficulties or exploring new fields, he did not work for long at a time. After an hour or two he would leave the subject as it were to grow of itself in the background and permeate his mind, while he was actively employed on something less exciting*. I may here mention that the high standard of completeness which he exacted from himself in his published writings, and which has been referred to on p. 78, added considerably to the effort with which his finished work was produced. The logical sequence of propositions, the absolute sufficiency of definitions, and the rigour of demonstrations, were all matters that exactly suited the quality of his mind; but his mode of working did not readily adapt itself to the laborious classification of the separate cases of a general theorem, or other details requiring merely industry and attention.

As his attention was not specially directed to mathematics until after his degree, he was in fact as regards its higher branches a self-made mathematician. It was during the long period of isolated study in which he familiarized himself with every formula in the greatest of the abstract Theories that his powers were developed and that his interest in mathematics grew into the almost passionate attachment of later years. Led on by pure fascination, under no pressure, but without either assistance or encouragement, he slowly and surely mastered everything that had been accomplished, and gained such an insight into the principles of the subject, and such a command over its methods, as could

---

* In an article in the *Fortnightly Review* for May, 1883, I wrote: 'His victories were won by the hardest of intellectual conflicts, in which for the time his whole heart and soul and powers were entirely and absolutely absorbed. It was in his wide interests and sympathies, the pleasure of intercourse with others, and the love of all that was good and cultivated, that he found relief from these severe mental efforts. Had he not been gifted with a disposition that gave him the keenest sympathy with every human interest, that attracted him to society and endeared him to his friends, that gave him, in fact, his other noble life—the life the world knew—his fierce devotion to the subject he loved would have ended his days long since.'

only have resulted from so long and complete a self-devotion. But one un-fortunate result of his comparative isolation was that he allowed too much of his own work to accumulate in manuscript, and that, the 'note' of personal ambition (as Lord Bowen described it) being wanting in his character, and no external stimulus prompting him, he remained indifferent to the advantages of **early publication, and was too little sensible of the difficulties that would stand in the** way of preparing for the press any work which has been too long on hand. **Thus, when** he was forty years of age, besides the Report, he had published only **one** important **memoir, although he was in** possession of an immense **amount of original work relating to** Quadratic Forms, Geometry, and Elliptic **Functions.**

The foundation of the London Mathematical Society in 1865 was an event which exercised a marked influence upon the subsequent course of all his work. He was a fairly regular attendant at the council and ordinary meetings, and there met other mathematicians who appreciated his unique **knowledge, and** urged him to bring papers before the Society. Wherever he was known he was a *persona grata,* but nowhere more so than at the Society's rooms in Albemarle Street. During his presidency he communicated nine papers to the Society (besides the Address), only four of which however were written out. As time went on, and engagements and duties thickened upon him, he became **more and more uneasy about the mass of work that lay unfinished in manu-script. In declining to undertake a fresh piece of work** he wrote: **'I have twenty papers embedded in my note-books. I extricated and published seven last year.' He** found it impossible to obtain the amount of consecutive leisure **that was requisite to complete long and difficult investigations; and he was** continually distracted between the fascination of new work **and** the desire to publish portions of the old. He would often say, 'I must bind my sheaves;' and only a few **days before his death he said to his sister, '**My mind is teeming **with new** ideas *.'

His power of reading rapidly the mathematical writings of others, seizing the **principles** and grasping the methods as if by intuition, always struck me as very remarkable. Up to the last, and **in spite of the** scanty allowance **of** time that

---

* Three months before his death, after the meeting at Cambridge for a memorial to the late Professor F. M. Balfour, referring to the opinion expressed by one of the speakers that a man's original ideas came to him before he was thirty, he **said to me** that in his own case he was certain that not only had his power of seeing and understanding increased without interruption all through his **life,** but that **his thoughts** and ideas and invention had undergone a corresponding progression **and** development.

he could devote to Mathematics, he continued to read new mathematical literature with the same ardour, and he never allowed the pursuit of his own work to prevent him from keeping abreast of what was being done by others, not only in his own departments of study, but also in other branches of the exact sciences.

I cannot refrain from devoting one brief paragraph to recording his admirable style and perfect taste when addressing a mixed scientific audience. Of this I recollect three remarkable instances : the first when he proposed the late Professor Tyndall as President of the British Association for the meeting at Belfast in 1874 ; the second when, in reply to Lord Grimthorpe, he spoke on the endowment of research, at a special meeting of the Royal Astronomical Society, in 1881 ; and the third at the Balfour Memorial meeting, which has just been alluded to. On the second occasion especially, I think that none who heard the speech are likely to forget the power and brilliance of the speaker.

He spoke so lightly, and often with such whimsical disparagement of his own attainments and performances, that even those who were conversant with the nature of his published writings and the varied character of his pursuits were frequently surprised to find how well acquainted he was with matters and subjects which would not have been thought likely to be of special interest to him. This was the case also in Mathematics ; and I can remember my own astonishment when, long after I knew him well, I accidentally discovered how familiar he was with every page of Jacobi's *Fundamenta Nova*. From the way in which the subject of Elliptic Functions was treated in his writings, I had not suspected that the *Fundamenta Nova* would have possessed so much attraction for him.

The following extracts from a letter addressed to the late Mr. Todhunter (in acknowledgment of some reprints of his papers) seem to be of sufficient interest to deserve preservation :

I have been also reading, and with great interest too, your 'Conflict of Studies.' I am afraid I am a shade less conservative than yourself. I have been led to entertain a somewhat higher impression of the value of experimental science, at least when the pupil is made to experiment himself. I am perhaps a little more willing than you are to consider favourably attempts to improve Euclid, though I have a great dread of the Association for the Improvement of Geometrical Teaching. Further (as I am a professor, and as there is nothing like leather), I am for having more professors, with more work, and more pay. But I so heartily agree with much, or rather with most of your book, that I should not have troubled you with this letter, if it were not that I cannot wholly subscribe to your estimate of the present state of Mathematics. All that we have, one may say, comes to us from Cambridge ; for Dublin has not of late quite kept up the promise she once gave. Further, I do not think that we have anything to blush for in a comparison with France ; but France is at the lowest ebb, is conscious that she is so, and is making great efforts to recover her lost place in Science.

Again, in Mixed Mathematics, I do not know whom we need fear : Adams, Stokes, Maxwell, Tait, Thomson will do to put against any list, even though it may contain Helmholtz and Clausius.

But in Pure Mathematics I must say that I think we are beaten out of sight by Germany; and I have always felt that the *Quarterly Journal* is a miserable spectacle, as compared with Crelle, or even Clebsch and Neumann. Cayley and Sylvester have had the lion's share of the modern Algebra (but even in Algebra the whole of the modern theory **of equations, substitutions, &c., is** French and German). But what has England done **in** Pure Geometry, in the Theory of **Numbers, in** the Integral Calculus ? What a trifle the symbolic methods, which have been developed in **England,** are compared with such work as that of Riemann and Weierstrass !

But it is with the younger, or at least the less-known, people that I feel the difference **most. Our** English papers are so often quite free from anything really new, whereas a German takes care **to know** what is known before he begins to work, and besides generally takes care to work at some **really im-** portant problem, and not at some trifling expression for the co-ordinates of the focus.

If I **had** room, I should vent my spleen (or perhaps my envy) by saying that I attribute the mis- chief to the business of problem-making : ninety per cent. of the good problems in Pure Mathematics that I see, are, if I mistake not, mere fragments of some great theory, of which the candidate is supposed to be ignorant.

In the last paragraph but one he refers to the want of a sufficiently important object in the papers of many English mathematicians. This was a subject which was often in his mind; and I have heard him more than once express his regret that so many writers, instead of attacking recognized difficulties or those parts of their subject where real advances might be expected, should be content to occupy themselves with developments of a comparatively trifling character. In connexion with the reference to Cambridge problems, I may mention that on one occasion, when I was telling him about a proposal to abolish the order of merit in the Mathematical Tripos, he said that in his opinion a system which was successful in extracting a great amount of hard work from the students should not (in spite of many drawbacks) be lightly abandoned.

My own friendship with Professor Smith arose in connexion with the interest I felt in some of the subjects in which he was an accomplished master, but it was not until he began to write the Introduction to the Theta Tables for me that I became intimate with him. The progress of this work naturally brought us into closer and more frequent contact. I used to meet him at the Mathematical and Astronomical Societies, often walking with him to the Athenæum Club at the close of the meetings, and we had long mathematical conversations at Cambridge when he came to the dinners of the Ad Eundem Club. When the memoir on the Theta Functions in its final form was passing through the press, we both read the proof-sheets, and at the same time he was sending me the Notes on Elliptic Transformation for the *Messenger* : I also had occasion to consult him on several mathematical and other questions;

and all these causes combined to produce a rapid interchange of correspondence during the last two years of his life.

It was not until I became really intimate with him that I had any idea of the intensity and earnestness of his devotion to Mathematics. Even among mathematicians he referred so gaily and with so light a heart to his own studies and pursuits that I have been almost startled to find, when alone with him, how engrossed he really was with mathematical researches, and how completely they possessed his mind and affections. He derived intense pleasure both from working at Mathematics and from the contemplation of its truths and processes ; and although he was undoubtedly anxious in the latter part of his life that what he had accomplished should not perish in his note-books, he seemed quite indifferent to the amount of recognition that was accorded to his published writings by his contemporaries * : in fact, the only word of impatience that, so far as I know, ever escaped him with reference to the slight attention that had been paid to his best work, was the sentence quoted in the private letter to myself on p. 70.

The last paper of which he gave a verbal account had for its title 'On a property of a small geodesic triangle on any surface' (p. 77), and was communicated to the Meeting of the British Association at York in 1881. The object of this note was to point out that if a, b, c are the sides of a small geodesic triangle, then the correction to be applied to the formula $a^2 = b^2 + c^2 - 2bc \cos A$ is $-\frac{4}{3}$ (Area)^2 × curvature.

I have no word to express the admiration and affection with which I regarded him myself. As regards his qualities and abilities, if I had not known him as I did it would have seemed to me incredible that such varied gifts and powers could be combined in the same person. All the assistance that I have ever received with respect to the direction of my own work, or the manner of conducting research, came from him, and I have never ceased to miss his advice and help : and more and more with each succeeding year. It will be long indeed before his place in Mathematics can be held by another ; but in the lives of those who were personally indebted to him the void can never be filled.

---

* In communicating a paper to the Mathematical Society he once had occasion to refer to some results contained in one of his memoirs in the Philosophical Transactions, and he playfully apologized for having ' to quote from a paper which he had no reason to think that any one had ever looked at.' His indifference to personal prominence or display of any kind was frequently shown at the meetings of the British Association, for whenever there was any pressure upon the limited time of the section, he always waived his own claims in favour of those of others.

It is always somewhat hazardous to quote from private letters (except for the sake of facts), as they so often give to strangers a very different impression from that conveyed to those who knew the writer personally. Still I am tempted to close this Introduction with a few extracts from letters which, though too trivial perhaps to deserve publication on their own account, are yet not without a certain interest in connexion with the published papers. All the extracts are from letters written to myself during the last two or three years of his life ; and most of them have been selected because they relate to the progress of the Introduction (or Memoir) on the Theta and Omega Functions and the Notes on Elliptic Transformation, with which he was occupied to the very last.

Oxford, 2 November, 1880.

I enclose the penultimate copy of the four θ-functions. The Society is reprinting its early numbers, and I have ordered fifty separate copies. There is an erratum in the note on p. 9, viz. it should be, I think, $\beta = \nu' - \nu$ not $\beta = \nu - \nu'$. This I have altered in the reprint.

The trodden worm will turn; and I feel sure that even Cayley will admit any defender of suffixes to all the privileges which appertain to the status of a worm. I therefore, speaking as a worm, declare that I do not in the least care for *suffixes*, but that any one who does not admit that a *double* notation is, for certain purposes, imperatively required by the circumstances of the case, is not fit to be an annulated animal at all, but only a mere zoophyte. I will, seriously, quite as willingly write $\Im\left(\frac{\mu}{\nu}, x\right)$, or $\Im(\mu, \nu; x)$, as $\Im_{\mu,\nu}(x)$; indeed to me it is a mere printer's question. But if I am told that $\Im_1, \Im_1, \Im_1, \Im_1$ (however convenient as abbreviations), or again $\Theta, H, \Theta_1, H_1,$ are as handy for use in general formulæ applying to all the four θ-functions, I am disposed to dissent. The Germans, I perceive, are great lovers of suffixes; and I confess that when I try to do without them, I soon want another alphabet.

Of course you are most welcome to do what you please with my paper : it will be much honoured by any use you may make of it. The 'Logic,' such as it is, you should have had long since, but that I sit seven hours a day, day after day, with our Commission. . . . It is my birthday and I am feeling very old.

The paper referred to is No. xvi (vol. i). I had accused him of exulting in the number and complication of the suffixes, and had said that the criticism of Professor Cayley (who disliked suffixes and avoided their use as much as possible) would be, 'Too many suffixes!' I was in the habit of giving the principal theorem of the paper in my lectures, and had asked for the separate copies, as the formulæ were unsuited for writing on the blackboard. I had also said that when, in printing my 'Lectures,' I came to the Theta Functions I wished to reproduce the whole of the paper just as it stood as a separate chapter. The 'Logic' was the paper whose title appears as No. 13 on p. 76. It had been promised for the *Messenger*.

Oxford, 5 June, 1881.

Best thanks ; only I have not time to express them. [He then refers **in detail** to some misprints.] It is very kind of you to take the trouble you have done about a wretched **little paper**, of which the only interest, if any, is that it applies Liouville's theorem to a question of convergence.... When I sent you the manuscript of my paper I had almost asked you to print (at the end of it) Riemann's proof of Abel's 'little theorem.' There would then have been a good tail **to a poor** little **thing; because** Riemann's **proof** is a model of what such a proof should be. (I notice Todhunter in his 'Laplace's Functions' **refers** a little contemptuously to the ' little theorem '—this **designation is mine**, not his;—and in this he is quite wrong, as I think the trigonometrical series at once shows.)

The paper referred to in this letter is No. xl (vol. ii.), 'On some discontinuous series considered by Riemann.'

Ryde, 15 July, 1881.

Alas ! I am not yet at the Elliptic Functions. **For three** weeks I was tied to my sofa in Oxford by a sprained thigh : and during that time I was exposed to continual interruptions, as in addition to the usual Oxford business at the end of term I had become (just at that time) executor of my dear friend Rolleston's will, and guardian of his children. . . Finding I could not be quiet enough to work at my Introduction to your Tables, I took up a very different bit of work, the Introduction to Clifford's Collected Mathematical Works. This is three-parts done, and must be finished next week early : indeed it would have been done long ago except that thinking about it takes me into space of many dimensions, &c. I grudge the time I am giving to it because I can say nothing on the one hand fit for mathematicians to read, nor on the other fit for non-mathematicians. So I have to maunder a good deal, which is neither acceptable to me nor suitable to my ideas of the right way of honouring Clifford's memory. I long to be at the Elliptic Functions, I can tell you.

If you think the *Messenger* would like a note of three pages on one or two points in Riemann's 'Hypotheses which lie at the basis of Geometry' (viz. on the only two results which he announces in formulæ), the said *Messenger* would be most welcome.

On another occasion, he said that this Introduction was inferior to the similar work which he had done in connexion with the writings of the late Professor Conington, and that it 'savoured of the sick couch on which it had been written.'

Oxford, 12 December, 1881.

I have stolen a few hours for the Elliptic Functions, chiefly to try and get my hand in again for work immediately after Christmas. (Till then I am liable to many interruptions.) I must rewrite the transformations of the second order ; I fear that nine of them must be given, viz. the nine which give different transformations of the *elliptic* functions.

Oxford, 7 February, 1882.

I have not seen you for a long time, and am afraid I am not likely to see you very soon. I am a close prisoner to my sofa with an inflamed vein in my thigh (gouty phlebitis, they call it). I hope I am beginning to get slowly better, but it will be a good bit of time before I am able to move about again. I have had to rewrite 'Transformations of the Second Order,' Art. 33, and while about it I have also made many changes in Art. 31 (' Linear Transformations of Elliptic Functions '). All this I could send to the printer if it were any good as yet for me to do so. I am not allowed to work very much, and I find I can only do rather easy things. But I think I am up to doing what remains to be done with the Memoir. It is horrible to me to think you should take any more trouble over the thing. And so I hope you will do no **more** than look through the proof-sheets very hastily indeed, if indeed you do as much as that.

I have been preparing a little 'paperlet' to show **(1) that the coefficients** a, b of the general elliptic transformation

$$y = \frac{x}{M} \frac{1 + a_1 x^3 + a_2 x^4 + \dots}{1 + b_1 x^3 + b_2 x^4 + \dots}$$

are rational in k^2 and λ^2, not only in u and v as they appear in Jacobi and **Cayley**; (2) that when λ^2 is an equal root of the modular equation, they are not rational (in general) in k^2 and λ^2 (viz. in this case Cayley's system of equations at the beginning of his memoir admits of more **than one solution**); (3) giving a new (slightly new) process for determining them which **shows that in all cases** (even of equal roots) they are rational in k^2 and λ^3 and $\frac{1}{M}$ (in the equal-root case, $\frac{1}{M}$ need not be rational in k^2 and λ^2). I had thought of bringing this to the Mathematical Society on Thursday; but finding such a journey out of my reach I am thinking of inflicting it on you for the *Messenger*. By the way, I will try and finish the little fragment of Logic for you. My difficulty is that I cannot get upstairs to my study and no one can find my papers for me.

Oxford, 22 February, 1882.

I am putting several interesting *little* things **together in the ' Notes on Transformation '** which I am writing for you.

Another extract from this letter has been given on p. 70.

Oxford, 9 March, 1882.

I am sorry to say that to-morrow I shall not be able to be at the Astronomical Society. I shall however probably venture up to London in order to go to the Meteorological Office, under a solemn promise to my doctors to be carried up and down stairs and do **nothing else**. So you see I am getting on, and if I am only patient I may soon hope to be about again.

I have just finished going over the revise of sheets 2, 3, 4; and am sending them to you at Cambridge. I am ashamed to have kept them so long. I find a few errata of my own, but none (I hope) to give much trouble to the printer. I am putting together several 'Notes on Transformation' for you. The paper is getting rather **larger** than I expected, because I have found two or three new (to me) little things while lying on **my sofa.**

Several of his friends were desirous that he should be nominated as the President of the British Association. The following is an extract from a reply to a letter of mine on this subject:

Oxford, 14 March, 1882.

I can tell you in a very few words what **I** feel about the Presidency of the British Association; indeed I do not know any one more **likely** to understand my feelings with regard to the matter than yourself. I should esteem the office a most horrid nuisance; at the same time I know my duty better to the British Association, to the University here, and to myself, than to refuse it if it were offered to me. For **the** honour (which I know to be a great one) I cannot bring myself to care (perhaps this is owing to a temporary weariness of the world, induced by lying on a sofa); but on the other hand I have a great horror of the indolence which induces one to refuse a position because the duties of it are irksome; and I think Dante was quite right to put the man in hell 'che il gran rifiuto fè' (I forget who he was, and what he declined). What makes me say that the position would be an unmixed nuisance, is that I have (by this time), in the University and out of it, had my full share of the sort of work which calls my mind away from the subjects which interest me most, and I am very anxious (before the evening closes in) to concentrate myself as much as I can. If I had to be President of the British Association, the best work of a year would have to be given to my address, and that is much more than I can afford. It would certainly be a sad interruption to my plans of work, and I should have a perpetual sense of unreality about it.

He afterwards said in conversation that the only scientific topics of general public interest upon which he could usefully discourse in a Presidential address were the motion of the atmosphere, the law of storms, &c.

Folkestone, 13 April, 1882.

I have been here for a fortnight, and can now limp about enough for purposes of business. I hope to meet you on Friday, and to have a few words on Mathematics with you then.

A quotation from a letter written a few days afterwards has been given on p. 71. The prize memoir was completed and sent off by the end of May.

Oxford, 30 July, 1882.

Have you returned from the United States? and, if so, when and where can we have a conference? I have been absolutely idle for thirty days at Royat in Auvergne, and have returned, a good deal better, I hope; but I am totally demoralized, and I feel as if I was too sleepy ever to do anything like a day's work again. However, I am now your slave, till I have accomplished my engagements with you (Introduction—that was—and *Messenger*). But my mental forces are in complete disarray, and you will have to use the whip severely to rally them.

Do you see that Lindemann has covered himself with immortal renown by proving the transcendentality of π? Of course, nine-tenths of the discovery is really Hermite's: but then Lindemann has the immense glory of having seen that Hermite's method could be applied to prove the transcendentality of π, when Hermite himself despaired of it. I have never examined Hermite's method closely, but taking his results for granted, Lindemann's reasoning *seems* all right. It is difficult not to envy, as well as admire, people who do such beautiful things: Lindemann's name is sure of a place in every history of mathematics hereafter [*].

---

[*] Nine years before (May 31, 1873) he had written to me: 'I am much pleased in particular with the way in which you call attention to the question of arithmetical irrationality. So far as π is concerned, I do not believe that any one has ever proved even so much as that π cannot be the root of an affected quadratic equation. And I always maintain that, until geometers have done this, they should not treat the problem of the rectification of the complete circumference as a *demonstrated* impossibility. Perhaps, however, the proof of the quadratic equation theorem may be obtained by Lambert's method. But this I have never tried.' Dr. Lindemann was the guest of Professor Smith (when I was so too) at the Oxford Commemoration in 1876.

Ryde, 20 August, 1882.

I have four of my notes nearly ready for you, and hope to finish them before I leave. They will make about eighty of my little pages; will this fill a number for you?

I have been led in Note II to your question about convergence of series like sin am u in powers of u. The only one giving any trouble is $\dfrac{u}{\sin\,am\,u}$; here the radius of convergence is the analytical modulus of K or iK'' or $K \pm iK''$, whichever of these four is least; and the question is to find the values of k^2 for which each of these is least.

I have put headings to the Memoir, but have not sent it off, having been absorbed, so far as I had time, in my 'Notes.' But I will send it before I leave.

On August 10 I had gone through the first seven sheets of the Memoir with him at the Athenæum Club.

Ryde, 23 August, 1882.

Can you let me have a figure in the *Messenger*? Here it is [*]. It is one of the modular curves of order 4; it divides the plane (as you see) into five regions. The *least* possible 'quarter periods' of sin am u are, if k^2 lies in 1, 2, ..., 5 (i. e. if the extremity of the vector k^2 lies in 1, 2, ..., 5), 1 . K, $\frac{1}{2} iK'$; 2 . $\frac{1}{2} iK'$, K; 3 . $\frac{1}{2} iK'$, $K \pm \frac{1}{2} iK'$; 4 . $\frac{1}{2} iK'$, $K \pm iK''$; 5 . $K \pm iK'$, $\frac{1}{2} iK'$, the $\pm$ sign being taken according as k^2 is below or above the axis. The absolutely least period is put first; of course K and K' are the rectilinear integrals, and **least** refers to absolute magnitude, i. e. to analytical modulus. Of course also there is a general theory relating to **transformation** to which this proposition belongs (it is in fact the theory of a problem which Jacobi touches on in the *Fundamenta Nova*, saying it is very difficult).

A more complete account of these results is given on pp. 411–413 of vol. ii.

The first portion of the manuscript of the 'Notes' was given to me at the meeting of the British Association at Southampton on August 29.

Margate, 8 September, 1882.

I return the proof. I am heartily ashamed of the state it is in. ... My excuse is that I pressed myself a little too much to deliver the manuscript to you at Southampton. I am very glad I did so, however, for I think that it would have taken a longer time if I had tried to revise it thoroughly in manuscript, even allowing for the time it will take the printer to go through it.

I think I have now made it hang together in an intelligible way. I confess that till I wrote out the pages, which I sent you from Spottiswoode's, I had imagined that, when the modular equation has equal roots, the multiplier might be a root (square or cube) of a rational function of k^2 and λ^2. But I found that what really happens is that the multiplier (when the roots are equal) still continues to be a rational function of k^2 and λ^2, but is a function of k^2 and λ^2 with irrational coefficients, viz. the coefficients contain an imaginary quadratic surd such as $\sqrt{-m}$, where m is a whole number; whereas in all other cases the coefficients are rational numbers. I had said nothing to contradict this; but some of my

---

[*] The figure represented a symmetrical closed curve, consisting of four loops, each of which included the next smaller one, and having three double points on the axis of x. The region '1' was the interior of the smallest loop, the region '2' the space interior to the next loop but exterior to the smallest, the region '3' the space interior to the next and exterior to the second loop, and similarly for the region '4'; the region '5' being the space exterior to the whole curve.

present alterations are made with a view to lead up to it. More of them however are made simply to make the meaning, and connexion, clearer. It all lies close to what is known, but I think it is full enough of now *little* things to make it fit for the *Messenger*.

I send all that I have received from you so that it ends abruptly. I ought to have before me this portion when I revise the remainder. Correcting this has taken me two and a half days of (for me) hard work. I return at once to Note II : but would you not prefer to follow up Note I with something else, and let Note II take its chance by and bye ? Notes I and II together would carry you nearly to the end of a third number ; and this would be dreary for your subscribers.

Please send a card to say you have received this and have not gone mad with indignation at the state of the proof.

London, 16 September, 1882.

I enclose the revise. Of course I need not see another revise, and I should think you need not, as Metcalfe might well be trusted to make the corrections. On Monday morning you shall have the manuscript of the remainder of Note 1. Of course I could not resist the temptation of re-scribbling it.

Enough of Note II to fill up the September number, and more, shall, if I can possibly manage it, be in your hands on Monday morning also.

London, 17 September, 1882.

I enclose the remainder of Note I, rewritten and made as tidy as I can.

As for Note II, a great part of it is nearly ready, but none of it quite. I will send you, very soon indeed, as much as you are likely to want—and more. I am sorry to tell you it will make more than a number and a half. Now this is intolerable, and I must divide it, for I will not take up three numbers running (even if you would let me, which, for your credit as an editor, I hope you would not). I think I can manage to divide it, though some of the beginning part is written solely with a view to the end. Till I get the September number of the *Messenger* safe in your hands I don't look at the Memoir : alas !

Oxford, 24 September, 1882.

Here is some more copy for Metcalfe. It will take him a good bit on into the October number. But now the worst of it is, that a lot more of Note II remains—I think twenty-five slips at least—and this is after my cutting off all about the absolutely least periods (with the curly cue curves), which I now propose to make into Note III (when you have got over the surfeit occasioned by Notes I and II). So that you see Note II, if allowed to run on, will take up nearly all, perhaps quite all, the October number. I cannot divide it into two Notes, because it really has a unity of its own, and the arithmetic of Arts. 2 and 3 (especially Art. 3) would be unmeaning (in a note on Elliptic Functions) without what follows. But there can be no objection to your dividing it in print, with a 'To be continued.' And this I should advise you to do. But I put myself wholly in your hands, and will do what you please. I think I could let you have the rest of Note II very soon. The *Messenger* must have as many lives as a cat, if it survives my Notes. Still I am prepared to maintain that the stuff in them is reasonably good, though by trying to be complete and exact I have become diffuse.

Brockham, 29 September, 1882.

I enclose the rest of Note II. There is not quite so much of it as it looks. Still I think it will run on pretty far into the October number. I have (as I said) left out the parts that would require a diagram or two.

If the London Mathematical Society are in want of food at their first meeting, I could give them an account of these omitted portions, which are to be Note III (when you allow such a thing to appear). This would also give me an opportunity of saying briefly what Note II comes to 'when it comes to be fired.'

The next thing that I shall do is to send you the revise of the Memoir, and to this I shall now stick till it is done; I shall begin at it this very evening.

If Metcalfe could, without putting himself out, send me the whole of Note II together, it would save time. But I have treated him abominably about Note I, and only hope that Note II will come out decently straight; there really are some things in it worth a moment's attention.

Brockham, 4 October, 1882.

I return the proofs. This time they are very clear, and Mr. Metcalfe will not be able to reproach me. A couple of references to Gauss and to my own Report have to be inserted.

I send with the proof a little fragment which comes in after the end of the August number, and before the beginning of the slips now sent to me. I also return the copy for the October number. All I shall want will be a revise (in pages) of the September number, and that will enable me to correct the part that comes out in October. I do hope, and I think it likely, that I shall not run quite to the end of the October number. I think I shall be more easily forgiven by your public, if they see that I really have come to an end, and that someone else is going ahead. . . .

All this interests me very much, because it turns on the theory of 'reduction' as applied to doubly periodic functions, and seems to me to excuse the amount of space I have made you give to it in the *Messenger*. I have still to make out whatever I can about the course of the curves P; but I fear this will not be much. I shall try (whenever Note III comes into existence) to put all this stuff into it. So Note III will want figures. My *hexagon*, curiously enough, had already been considered by Dirichlet; not, of course, in relation to Elliptic Functions, but in proving Gauss' famous theorems about the minimum value of a ternary definite quadratic form.

The concluding paragraph relates to the limits of convergence of a series for arg sn x, about which I had consulted him. He took great interest in the question, and several letters were entirely devoted to it.

The portion that was written of Note III, referred to in the last three letters, appears as No. X of the 'Notes' (vol. ii, pp. 408–414).

Abergavenny, 7 October, 1882.

I enclose the revise; I see there is one page over, to run on into the October number . . . Your remark as to the complexity of the result in the case of the **value of** the series for arg sn x, has made me begin to doubt whether I am really right in saying that one of the branches of the three-forked curve of discontinuity does really enter the circle of convergence. If it does the nature of things is a fool; if it does not, I am a fool; the latter hypothesis seems to me the more probable, and I gladly embrace it. Besides, I begin to see dimly a weak point in my demonstration. If only the curve can be coaxed into staying outside the circle the result will be the simplest possible, viz. that the series, when convergent, always gives the least value possible.

It was on the 12th of October that I went over all the manuscript of the 'Notes' at the Athenæum Club with him (p. 68).

Oxford, 31 October, 1882.

At last I return the revise. I dare say it is full of blunders of mine, and is peppered over with printer's errata, but I cannot find any more than I have marked.

If the alteration of the note on p. 88 and the rearrangement on p. 89 are troublesome, it would not be ruinous if they were left alone. *Item*, on p. 96 the signs in lines 2 and 3 are not very wrong as they stand, and might be left as they are; I have now made them correspond exactly with the 'elementary matrices of Art. 3'; as they stand, they do not.

I am very sorry to have kept you waiting so long. I comfort myself by thinking that the number has not been expected with great impatience by any one.

Oxford, 7 November, 1882.

I am almost sorry you took the trouble of sending me a revise. When I returned the proof I had intended to tell you that you might print it straight off. The small world that reads the *Messenger* will give an audible sigh of relief when they come to p. 99, and find there is no more of me. However, you will have, within a year or so, to print Note III, and some figures with it. That done I absolve you from all further Notes on Elliptic Functions, and if I ever write them, I will inflict them on the London Mathematical Society, or the *Quarterly Journal*, or on the new Scandinavian journal, or on Sylvester's Journal, or on any one but you.

London, 30 December, 1882.

Do you happen to have a copy of the sheet pp. 423–431 that you could send me? I have two, but the printer could hardly make them out. I mean now to do nothing but proofs for a long time. I have the two sheets which follow those now printed off practically ready, and there is nothing to cause delay for a long time to come.

Oxford, 20 January, 1883.

I enclose four more sheets of the Memoir: the rest (as far as set up in 4to) will follow immediately. I am sorry to say that the first two of the sheets I send have had to undergo great alterations. This will not happen with any of the remaining sheets. I should be very glad to have, as soon as you can, the manuscript which is in your hands set up. For the next three or four months I can give a great deal of time to this work, and hope (D.V.) to bring it to a close.

Oxford, 1 February, 1883.

Best thanks for your letter. I cannot be at the R. A. S. to-morrow. . . . I have returned to the printers four sheets of the Memoir for revise—but this includes the sheet which really has to be set up again, and made, I should think, into two. I find the stuff (now that I have quite forgotten it) more intelligible and hanging together better than I supposed. I find many little slips of mine and some of the printers', but very few great blunders so far. It takes an enormous amount of time to go through it. I must write to you before the week is over about *figures*, and about completing, or rather shutting up, the whole thing: there are now 136 pp.; I *think* it will run to about 170, or a little over. Please regard this letter as not needing any answer. I shall see you on the ninth.

These were the last words I was to hear from him. The 9th of February was the anniversary meeting of the Royal Astronomical Society, and I entered the Society's rooms expecting to meet him, and go over some of the sheets of the Memoir in the way that had become habitual to us; but Mr. Stone, who had just arrived from Oxford, told me that he had died at seven o'clock that morning.

J. W. L. GLAISHER.

www.ingramcontent.com/pod-product-compliance
Lightning Source LLC
Chambersburg PA
CBHW020807020726
47495CB00008B/2624